because barbecakes!

THE
DO-OVER

a Finding Home novel

Melissa McClone

D1512027

THE
DO-OVER

a Finding Home novel

MELISSA MACKINNON

Entangled Publishing, LLC
10940 S Parker Rd
Suite 327
Parker, CO 80134
rights@entangledpublishing.com

Bliss is an imprint of Entangled Publishing, LLC.

Edited by Robin Haseltine
Cover design by Bree Archer
Cover photography by PeopleImages/Getty Images

Manufactured in the United States of America

First Edition July 2021

Bliss
an Entangled imprint

Content Warning

The Do Over is a heartwarming romance with two at-odds main characters. However, the story includes elements that might not be suitable for some readers. Cancer, a child with a disability after a car accident, mentions of a car accident, mentions of a violent relationship and alcoholism, parental death, and mentions of childhood parental neglect are included in the novel. Readers who may be sensitive to these elements, please take note.

To my grandparents,
Abe and Mary.
I'll be seeing you.

Chapter One

Two men—her fiancé and her husband—had walked out on her over the course of a day. That had to be some kind of new record.

Forty-eight hours ago, Maggie Kelley was living it up in Los Angeles, about to tie the knot, and now she was... *Where was she*? Maine?

She'd flown across the country to try to sort this out amicably with her...husband, and all she'd received in return was a fantastic view of his back as he walked out of his workshop, leaving her standing there wondering what had just happened.

A marriage and a divorce in forty-eight hours, with two different men, down the drain.

How had she reached this point in life, where her world was crashing down around her and she hadn't even noticed?

She'd been too busy trying to further her career by finding a fiancé who could give her the push she'd needed. Winston Fisher was a man of business, and that was what their engagement had been. Convenient, and a good opportunity for them both. He had money, and she had skills to deal with the people who wanted that money.

So she'd entered the brightly lit workshop of Garrity Boatworks an hour ago, the buzzing of power tools assaulting her ears. A fine layer of sawdust enveloped everything in its wake, right down to the threshold she stood in. Aromatics, both sweet and spicy—of man-sweat and singed wood—bit at the insides of her nostrils. When the drone of a sander died down, she'd taken the opportunity to call out to whoever was hiding in the shop.

"Is Finnegan Garrity here?"

A man surfaced from behind the propped-up bow of a boat. "Present," he'd said, advancing farther from his burrow. He'd lazily leaned on the beams he was working on, sander in one hand and a beer in the other. "How can I help you, ma'am?"

Oh God. There it was. That accent. Exotic and unfamiliar to her ears, and it made her legs turn to jelly. Heady, thick, and smooth, with the hint of a faint Irish lilt, his voice was like drowning in a dark ale.

Finn stepped down from the boat, an eyebrow arched as he stared at her expectantly. With his work boots unlaced, oil-stained Carhartt jeans, and works-well-with-his-hands confidence, he looked like something straight out of a *Men's Fitness: Mountain Men Edition* magazine. Tall, rugged... delicious. Dark hair, a bit too long, like he needed a haircut two cuts ago. It curled playfully at the ends along his nape and around the ears.

Her fingers tingled at the remembrance of tangling themselves in those curls so many years ago. She hadn't known what to expect, seeing him after all these years. All she had to go on were eight years of fading memories, a boyish charm not even a drunken stupor could make her forget, and a pair of amber eyes etched in a dream. A lot could change in eight years.

He did not disappoint.

A dark, scruffy beard covered the strong lines of his chin and jaw, and at least a week's worth of I-don't-care-enough-to-shave growth lined his upper lip, almost hiding that incredibly kissable Cupid's bow curving up into a flirtatious half smile. The gray tee he wore bordered on too tight and showcased all the right places. Bits of the day's work clung desperately to the fabric hinting at what lay underneath, and—judging by the sweaty discolorations on the front outlining every chiseled line of the male form—a six-pack she could bounce a quarter off.

Memories and images of him during their very short escapade together had flooded her thoughts. Since then, she'd put her wild rebellious days behind her and had suppressed everything Finn Garrity–related. Even that Vegas wedding chapel, apparently.

Speak. Maggie sucked in a breath. "A divorce would be nice. It… It would be quite helpful, actually." Her heart pounded.

Finn shifted his weight, taking a small step back. His breathing hitched, and he reached out to support himself on a nearby beam. "Son of a bitch," he whispered.

"Hello. I'm M—"

"I know who ya are," he interrupted. He stood there, silent, while they stared at each other in some awkward game of *who would break eye contact first.* Then finally he spoke. "Wanna tell me why you're in my shop right now asking for something you took care of years ago?"

"Yeah. About that…" She swallowed against the lump in her throat. "There seems to have been a slight mix-up." And that was putting it lightly. "I made a mistake." *In more ways than one.*

He chuckled, running his palm along his nape. "Did ya,

now?"

"Yes." She straightened. "It has recently been brought to my attention that we—you and I—may still kinda sorta be married. To each other." She cringed. "But I'm fixing it," she quickly added. "All you need to do is sign some papers and I'll be out of your hair, and it'll be like this never even happened." His face paled for a brief moment, and Maggie eyed him nervously. "Are you okay?"

He flexed his hands, carefully setting down the sander, then took a long swig from the bottle, finishing its contents. "No," he coughed. "Not okay. I'm pretty far from it right now. Jesus… I signed the annulment papers. I left them *right there* on the nightstand at the hotel. All you had to do was file them within twenty-four hours. You said you'd take care of it."

"*You* said you were taking care of it, not me. I left your room the next morning, and you were gone. I assumed you took those stupid papers with you." She took a step closer, trying to bridge the awkward gap between them.

"I went for coffee. The sobering stuff."

"Look, I vaguely remember what happened that weekend. I remember meeting you. I remember talking into the morning hours. I remember the *sex*." She chuckled awkwardly for even admitting that. "But I also remember shots, and Jell-O…and the details are a bit fuzzy after that."

"Yeah, well, vodka will do that to ya." Finn let out a heavy sigh, ripping Maggie from her thoughts. He held out his hand, waving his fingers at her. "Give me the papers, and I'll sign right now. Done."

Could this get any worse? "I don't have them yet." Truth be told, she still needed a lawyer practicing in Maine in order to file. Even with her L.A. connections, she couldn't pull one of those out of a hat overnight. Her father's lawyer would be calling soon with information regarding a qualified attorney, and all would be well. In and out. Easy-peasy.

Finn shook his head. He ran his fingers through his model-esque hair and then smiled. "This is unbelievable." Gravel crunched and popped under the weight of a vehicle outside. He glanced at his watch. "Oh, this isn't happening. Look, I have to go take care of something. Can you stay here for like, five minutes? Please?" He brushed past her, exiting the workshop.

Finn was taller than she remembered and the drop-dead gorgeous body he was rocking made her uncomfortable. Her lady parts betrayed her. They told her to do naughty things with this man and forget about California. Finn wasn't anything like the man she had been engaged to, and this was a social call. But still, she wanted to do *all the things*.

And that was wrong.

So, so wrong.

Chapter Two

Finn downed the rest of his beer, then set the empty bottle on a stack of wood near the door as he exited the workshop. Its lukewarm frothiness offered no relief against his parched throat.

He'd resigned himself to never seeing Maggie again and was at peace with the secrets of his past. What happened in Vegas stayed in Vegas. What he and Maggie had had was a one-weekend-night stand. So why, then, was his heart racing at the speed of NASCAR?

How had he even kept it together in there? Maggie was gorgeous. She had been perfection then—dark-red hair rolling down her back like the ocean waves he craved, eyes that pierced through him rivaling the bluest of skies. The same leaping of his stomach he had when he first saw her all those years ago returned full force. The amusement park ninety-degree vertical drop coaster had nothing on his insides.

Thoughts...fleeting moments, the past, cluttered his mind.

What had he done to deserve this second chance? Did

he tell her about the time he flew to California to find her a few months after Vegas? That he'd quickly learned how different their worlds were when he was standing on the sweeping staircase of her family mansion, terrified, because the realization punched him in the gut just how much they didn't suit each other?

Instead of a cheery Maggie, he'd found her father, received an angry earful and a few meaningful threats, and returned home with his tail between his legs. He'd been too young and dumb to stand up for himself, and he'd taken to heart every word her father had yelled at him. Her father had been right, though. Maggie wasn't the girl for him then. They came from two different worlds. It had gutted him, but he'd moved on. Or so he thought. In a strange twist of fate, she'd found *him*.

To make matters worse, his younger, always-up-in-his-business sister, Tess, was pulling up the drive. With his grandmother—the biggest meddler and gossiper Rockport had ever known.

He could only hope Maggie would stay inside the shop until he could get rid of his nosey sister. It would save both of them the humiliation of being drilled with an unwanted game of twenty questions.

Right on cue, Miss California Socialite exited the shop. Thankfully, she lingered next to the door.

Tess parked her beater of a truck next to his Jeep and greeted him with a smile. "Hey, Nana wants to go to the Rockport Diner for lunch today, so I told her I'd bring her by to visit while I was out. I hope that's okay." She rounded the back of the truck to the passenger-side door and opened it for their grandmother.

"Hi, Nana," he greeted, squinting against the bright sun. "You look radiant today." Even in her upper years, his grandmother always looked her best, like every day was

Sunday.

"Oh, hush it, Finn, and come give this old woman a kiss before she dies and you miss your chance." She held out her arms, waiting for him. "At my age, it's the only action I'm gonna get."

Not a man to ever deny his Nana the love and attention she deserved, he wrapped her slim frame in his arms and held her tight. After his mom had died when he was young, she'd stepped in to raise Tess and him without hesitation.

He planted a kiss on her pink-rouged cheek. Nana had been there for him through everything...except the debacle with Maggie.

No one in the family, not even his precious Nana, knew about Maggie, about Vegas, or the marriage based solely on a dare. For four days, her group of girls had tagged along with his group of guys—something having to do with a twenty-first birthday—the overall details of those nights were sketchy— and his group obliged, because *hot girls*. The drinks were free and flowing, and Maggie was a hellcat. Then there was the Vegas bucket list. Someone came up with a double-dog dare for a member of the opposite sex, which of course, completely exploded into something wild and out of control.

Dance topless on a bar. Check. Kiss a stranger, with lots of tongue. Check. Eat straight from the buffet with the giant serving spoon while mooing like a cow. Check it off. Stand up on the Ferris wheel while in motion. Sex in public.

The drunker they got, the raunchier the dares became. At one point, someone had the bright idea they should stop the flirting and grinding on each other and get married. Just for the night. Just for fun. Nothing serious. Just because they could.

She said she wasn't one to turn down a dare—especially one of such epic proportions, and it was *on*.

Challenge accepted.

She proposed to him down on one knee and gave him a ring made from the paper wrapper of a bottle from the minibar. Without hesitation, he shouted, "*Yes!*" above the bells of the slot machines. Finn had fallen head over heels for that woman within the first five minutes of meeting her. Maggie had been the best four days of his life.

Nana kissed his cheek and slipped her arm around his. "I hope you don't mind taking me out for my chowder. I feel like I haven't seen you in days, and I need to take advantage of that Thursday senior discount." She wiggled her brows at him. Needed to take advantage of the old biddies gossiping was more like it. Always up to no good. While he played along with her poor-old-me antics no one actually believed, deep down he knew he would miss them when she was no longer with him. A thought he didn't want to linger on, ever.

"I can see this isn't a good time. I didn't mean to intrude, so… Should I call you?" That sweet voice echoing behind him filled him with instant regret for leaving Maggie in his shop.

Nana perked up, stopping in her tracks between him and his Jeep. A woman at his shop was like a dinner bell for Nana. Fresh meat. His sister also stopped to stare, slowly closing her truck door to watch Maggie like a velociraptor stalking its prey.

He had to admit, she was a vision. Legs for days and a smile that would brighten even the darkest of nights. That tight skirt hugged the wicked curves of her ass and the thin material of her shirt left nothing to the imagination when the ocean breeze kicked up. Pert nipples hid behind a pale-colored tank and for an instant, he racked his brain in an attempt to recall just what they looked like free of fabric. Still amazing, he'd wager.

"Oh, I'm sorry, Finn. I didn't realize you were working. We can do lunch some other time." Nana squeezed his arm. "I don't want to be a bother."

"Not business-related, Nana."

She smoothed her knotted fingers over her whitened hair. "Pleasure, then?"

Finn swore he saw the devil flash in Nana's eyes.

This wouldn't end well.

He stared at the ground, unable to answer. A heat flushed over his face. There was no brushing this off. He'd walked right into his grandmother's trap, and now she awaited an introduction. Acquaintance? Client? Friend? *Wife*? Crap.

Nana made the first move. She was gliding toward Maggie, rushing right by him. There was no stopping her. "Oh my." Her attention flew to the enormous rock ensemble weighing down Maggie's ring finger. Jesus, it was huge. And it certainly wasn't from him. "Would you look at that diamond! It's gorgeous!" She wiggled Maggie's ring finger. "This little piggy went to Tiffany's!" Nana's grin came as a crushing blow to Finn. Like he'd ever be able to afford such a luxury.

Maggie had someone else. No wonder she needed those damn papers—she couldn't very well marry Mr. Big Shot Diamond Man while still married to a carpenter. Maggie had moved on. Well, it *had* been eight years, and they weren't a permanent thing. They had never been a *thing*. What did he expect? Certainly not the pang of jealousy creeping into his heart. Someone out there got to kiss those lips, run their fingers through that hair, and grab fistfuls of that fine ass.

"It's absolutely stunning, my dear. Congratulations."

"Thank you. I'm still getting used to it," she told his Nana when she held Maggie's hand higher to catch the glimmering sun. Laser-esque beams of light gleamed in all directions off the four-stone setting. It was ginormous compared to her petite fingers, and he wondered just what the purchaser was compensating for. Maggie turned toward him, a brief look of uncertainty settling on her brow, and it dawned on him that she had no clue who this woman joyfully fawning over her was.

"Nana, this is Maggie Kelley. Maggie, this is my grandmother, Eloise. And that's my sister, Tess." He waved in the general direction of his sister, who was leaning against the bumper of her truck with her arms crossed.

Nana's eyes narrowed. "I thought you said your girlfriend's name was Michelle?"

"Oh, I'm—" Maggie started, but Nana cut her off.

"From New York, right? Well, whatever it is, I'm so happy to finally meet you." She wagged a crooked finger at Finn. "It's about time you brought her round to meet the family. All those trips to the city and not once could you bring her back with you? Made the poor thing drive all this way by herself?" Nana clucked, shuffling closer to him. "And to see you popped the question! After only three months! It *must* be true love."

For a moment, Finn was sure his Nana had seen straight through his fake-girlfriend white lie, and this was just another trick up her sleeve aimed at getting him to settle down, but her scowl faded and was replaced with a soft smile. "Oh, I can die happy now. I never thought I was going to live to see my grandbabies have babies." Nana embraced Maggie with such sincerity and love, he didn't dare correct her. He let out a sigh. Up to no good or not, he had really mucked up this whole thing.

Nana retreated from the embrace and stared at him. "Did I just ruin the entire announcement? Have you not told anyone yet? Oh, were you saving it for the family dinner tomorrow? You'll be there, right? To meet everyone?" She wiped a visible tear from the corner of her eye. "I'm sorry, I'm just so happy!" She waved the two of them closer and attempted to squeeze both Maggie and him in her arms, but settled for hearty arm pats. "I finally have a reason to keep on living," she whispered. She dabbed the skin under her eyes.

Was that a wink? Did Nana just wink at him?

Oh, this wouldn't end well at all—informing her of this huge misunderstanding would certainly break her. It would probably kill her.

Finnegan Garrity would kill his grandmother. Cause of death...a shattered heart. She looked so happy. Although now would have been the best time to correct the mistake, for some selfish reason he chose to keep his mouth shut. Nana was excited, Maggie was in his life again—no matter how briefly—and for a day or two, who would it hurt?

Relationships failed. Fact of life. He could say it didn't work out after Maggie was back on her merry way with her precious divorce papers, back to whatever pretentious asshole had purchased that ring, and no one would ever know.

"You *will* be joining us for lunch, won't you?" Nana tugged on Maggie's hand, leading her closer to the Jeep. "We have so much to talk about! There's the church, where you're having the reception...and flowers. What is your color scheme, dear? Finn, I hope you don't mind."

"I, uhh..." He scratched his beard. "I need to lock up."

Maggie shot him a death glare. "Could I speak to you for a moment, Finn? In private?"

He nodded, motioning for her to follow him while he locked his shop. Out of earshot of his grandmother and sister, he said, "Don't you *dare* kill my Nana."

"What is going on, and why does your Nana think I'm Michelle? Who is Michelle?" She raised an eyebrow and attempted to stifle a wicked smile. Clearly, she enjoyed watching him squirm under the watchful eye of his grandmother.

"My girlfriend. Who my Nana now thinks is you." Finn retrieved a set of keys from his pocket and locked the deadbolt. "I think."

"No one has ever met your girlfriend?" She covered her

mouth with her fingers.

"No. I met her through an online dating site. I go see her when I make deliveries to New York. It wasn't a serious thing. Well, until Nana saw that huge-ass rock on your finger and got some wicked ideas in her head." Totally believable. The fact that *Michelle* didn't exist was one he hoped to never bring up. Ever. After being pestered continuously by everyone in his life about settling down and starting a family, he'd said the first female name that had come to mind just to get his family off his back. *Why is a catch like you still single? Don't you want to get married? I'll introduce you to my friend's sister's cousin's uncle's daughter.* They meant well, but the nagging wasn't helping his love life. Or the lack of one. "You're engaged." The words blubbered from his mouth.

"No." She simply stated.

He palmed his nape. "You're not engaged?"

"I'm single. Newly."

"But you still wear the ring? Isn't it customary to give it back to the guy or something?" He fiddled with the key, which liked to stick in the keyhole at the most inopportune times.

"We broke up because of you." She rubbed the shank of the ring with her finger, toying with it. Contemplating it.

"He knows about me? That we're still—" Still married. He understood now.

"It was best for both of us to go our separate ways. It's a long story, but when we went to apply for the license we found out I was already married. *That* was fun. I haven't taken the ring off, because I didn't want certain people to know we'd called off the engagement. I just didn't want to deal with the disapproval. So...single. Very much single." She sighed, closing her eyes briefly in what he assumed was an attempt to compose herself.

She made it sound as though being single was the worst

curse in existence. "Well, by now, all of my family in the surrounding five counties thinks *we're* engaged. My Nana is pretty stealthy with the group texts."

Maggie pursed those ruby-red lips, crossing her arms tightly over the fitted shirt hugging her curves. "Your Nana seems pretty stealthy with a lot of things. You couldn't have corrected her?"

"You saw how fast it happened, and that woman is the world to me. I couldn't break her heart. You heard her. Now, she has a reason to live"—he sighed, waving his arms dramatically in front of him—"and if I tell her, she's going to keel over and die. I don't know about you, but I can't kill my grandmother. Not today, at least. She's so over-the-top sometimes I don't know whether I believe her or suspect an ulterior motive."

"I think it's the latter this time. So what do you want me to do?" She looked at him, all pissed off and beautiful.

It pained him to say it. "Would you be my Michelle? Just for today? I'll tell her after you've gone. *Please?*" Was he actually pleading? This was a first for him.

Her lips twitched. "You want me to pretend to be your girlfriend?"

"Yes."

"Michelle? From New York?"

She was teasing him. "*Yes.*"

She smiled. "But my name's Maggie. From California."

He put the keys back in his pocket. "So I'm a guy who can't get a girl's name right."

"What do I get out of it?" The corner of her mouth curved up into the makings of a smirk. *Such a goddamned tease.*

He shifted. "Your divorce. Nice and quietly."

"You're not going to sign the papers otherwise?" She paused, then tucked an errant lock of hair behind her ear.

"I could put one of those ads in the newspaper, if you

want. Make it official and all that. I think that's how an out-of-state divorce is decreed. I mean, I'd have to look it up, but I know a reporter or two down at the *Gazette*, and I'm sure they could help me out."

Her eyes raked over him, darting back and forth, and a flicker of panic settled itself behind the wall she'd built up around her. "All right," she said softly.

He breathed a sigh of relief. He didn't know what he'd expected her to say, but that hadn't been it. He'd expected her to run kicking and screaming from his lies, but...that wasn't the Maggie he remembered. She would swear the Earth was flat, if only to prove him wrong. *That* was his Maggie.

Nana's voice echoed in the background. "Come on, you two lovebirds, you can make googly kissy faces over lunch. I'm hungry!"

"Not awkward at all," Maggie muttered.

Chapter Three

A lump formed in Maggie's throat and she swallowed hard against it. Being a convincing girlfriend would require PDA and all that mushy stuff she wasn't at all comfortable with around Finn. Being near him for an undetermined length of time could be dangerous. Just looking at him could do her in. The way those amber eyes studied her in such earnest. Understood her, saw right through her guarded exterior, but chose compassion instead of telling her secret. The way he carried himself—the subtle confidence was sexy as hell. He wanted her to pretend to want him? It wasn't pretending when those thoughts and feelings swirling around inside her were real. It scared her in a way her relationship with Winston never had.

Winston was...duty. A tradition she was expected to uphold—to marry into *old money*. His family had the clout her father wanted, and their wedding had been planned around his vacation time. His family had the clout her father wanted, and their wedding had been planned around his family's vacation time. She called it *senatorial off-season*. She would never admit it if asked, but when she'd been informed there'd be no wedding until she could produce divorce papers, it was a relief she'd never felt before. The pressure from all sides had been overpowering. She just needed more time to figure herself out.

She hadn't known it at the time, but Finn was *that* guy no one else would ever be able to live up to. True book-boyfriend material. Sweet, fun, engaging, actually cared about what she had to say. She'd hoped she'd find that with Winston when she'd agreed to marry him due to social pressure, which had made sense at the time. It was only logical they could help each other accomplish their career goals. The spark wasn't there, but perhaps, with more time, they'd grow to find it. But now, there was no chance of that *ever* happening—Winston had solidified that. He had shown her his true colors, and she had called him on his bluff. No wedding? You got it. Done deal. Romance had never been in the cards for Winston and her.

There was no denying an attraction to Finn was still there. If anything, he'd only gotten better-looking with age. That *man* could do wondrous things to her—things she hadn't felt in a long, long time. And those hands. Sweet baby Jesus, she'd pay good money to feel them burning against the small of her back just once more. Calloused and rough. The thought of them running up her thighs sent a spark shooting up her spine.

The Vegas sex had been the best she'd ever had—she remembered *that*, of all things, because hello, mind-blowing—and no other guy had ever quite been able to live up to it. Vegas Finn had quite literally charmed the pants off her in the back seat of a taxi after a long night of binge drinking and lewd behavior. God, he was amazing.

A day. An afternoon, really. That's all he asked for. A little hand-holding and smiling wouldn't hurt…if that's what it took to keep sweet Nana from having a coronary. Besides, it would take a day or two to get the papers filed anyway, so why not help the guy out? She was a big girl. She could control herself, right?

He was saving her ass—she could help save his.

Maggie approached the off-road vehicle with apprehension. Anything missing doors and brandishing a roll cage caked in inches of dried mud definitely didn't seem like her first choice for transportation when she'd driven herself there in a perfectly safe—and complete—rental car. With all four doors still attached. Nana Eloise didn't seem fazed a bit as she hefted herself up into the passenger seat with a bit of help from Finn and his deliciously sinful muscles.

Tess, commenting on how work could wait and she didn't want to miss this lunch, climbed into the shotgun seat in front of Nana. Finn jingled the keys in his palm and stood waiting for Maggie.

Had she suddenly shrunk? The running board height-to-width ratio seemed to narrow right before her eyes. She took a deep breath, gathered her nerves, and attempted to take a step up.

Nothing happened. Did her leg even bend? She still had both knees, right? Between the formfitting skirt and the four-inch heels there would be no stepping up in any form for Maggie. Not without disrobing. And that wasn't on her immediate to-do list. She bit the corner of her lip. "Are you sure we can't take my car?"

"Is mine not good enough for you?"

"I'm sure it's great. It's just, well…" *How embarrassing.* "I can't get in it." She couldn't look at him, and he stifled a laugh. "Not without a set of stairs, some Crisco, and a pair of scissors."

"Would you like some help?"

"Don't think I have a choice." She couldn't help but

notice how he stared at her. Couldn't take those liquid pools of honey off her. Or her ass. And that needed to stop. *Now.* When he offered his hand, she was hesitant to take it. She'd done all right keeping her distance and her composure during this whole ordeal, but Maggie couldn't determine what would happen if she actually touched him. She thought of Winston, of the ugliest, nastiest online zit-popping video she could think of, anything to keep her mind from double-crossing her. But it did anyway.

Finn wrapped one arm around her waist and swooped her off her feet with the other. He adjusted his grip, sliding the arm around her waist, precariously low toward her butt cheeks. He looked as though he had a thousand things to say but couldn't find the words, which is exactly how she felt as he effortlessly cradled her against his chest. His heart pounded, its erratic beat reverberating deep to her core. A sudden chill whipped along the length of her arms and legs when his fingers dug at her flesh. She sucked in a breath she couldn't seem to catch. "Your hand is on my ass," she whispered.

"Mm-hmm."

"I would like to get in the car now," she breathed, half-heartedly making an attempt to not lose herself in the flecks of green surrounding the inner ring of his irises. "Finn?"

"Yeah?"

"*Michelle* would like to get in the car now." Muscles grew taut as he sidestepped closer to the door and lowered her enough to where she could step into the back of the Jeep. As she avoided an empty water bottle and the roadside assistance kit, a warm palm gently curved around her hip and settled back on her left butt cheek, which was protruding from the vehicle. "Hand is *still* on the ass."

"Yep." Finn gave her a little swat.

Nope. Not awkward at all. She took her seat next to Nana and fumbled for the seat belt...harness. The Lord help her if she needed it.

Finn pulled himself up into the driver's seat, clicked his seat belt into place, and roared the Jeep to a start. Gravel spat from the tires as he wove his way down the drive.

Garrity Boatworks was something pulled straight from a Norman Rockwell painting. Down a secluded dirt road off the harbor and around the corner from the marina, a tree-lined drive canopied over them as they drove. Boats of various sizes littered the grounds—some on trailers, others resembling ocean leftovers covered in what looked like white Saran wrap. Picturesque.

A bitter chill whipped through her. Grabbing her cardigan from her car was a distant afterthought as Finn tore down the twisting turns of the sleepy little ocean village of Rockport, Maine. Contrasting hues of reds and muddled browns whooshed by her at lightning speed while she attempted to control her wildly whirling hair. Driving with the top down—or altogether missing, in this case—had never really appealed to her for this exact reason. Hair chaos. The inevitable beehive of tangles would be hell to comb out.

Seagulls cawed in the distance, barely audible over the engine as Finn shifted gears. The roads intertwined and turned along the rocky coastline. Old boats turned lawn ornaments littered the tiny yards of hodgepodge houses lining the nooks and crannies of hilly terrain. Maggie inhaled a deep breath of sea-salted air. Refreshing and clean. So clean. And not a skyscraper to be found. It was breathtaking. She closed her eyes as the wind rushed over her face, content to inhale the sweet smells of the pines and blooming spring flowers. This was the way life should be. No constant hum of traffic. No six-lane highways to navigate. The promise of warmer weather lingering on the ocean horizon.

Finn pulled into the nearly full parking lot of the Rockport Diner. Off the main road and surrounded by lush trees, it stood steadfast and inviting. People filed through the front door. The diner seemed to be a favorite with young and old alike. A sign out front boasted they carried the best seafood in the MidCoast. That was promising, if only Maggie ate meat—she'd become a vegetarian at the age of eight after reading *Charlotte's Web*. She remembered being terrified Wilbur the pig would be eaten with each turn of the page. It had scarred her for life.

Finn parked and cut the engine. He helped her down, offering his hand. She slipped her palm into his and her breathing wavered. Shocking white heat shot up from her fingertips. She tightened her grasp for a moment, then made herself let go. Maggie released a breath through pursed lips. That had been…unexpected.

"Hey, you coming?" He waved her onward.

Everyone was staring at her.

Off in her own little world, she'd failed to realize the other occupants of the speed-demon mobile had continued on without her. "Yes, sorry. I was just umm… Let's eat."

She hurried to catch up with the others, tucking her Vuitton bag under her arm and feeling like the annoying third wheel who didn't know they were the third wheel. A playful breeze tugged at the hem of her petite pencil skirt and gravel crunched beneath her heels as she picked her steps carefully. A wave of nerves swept over her, rivaling the nearby churning water of the harbor. Face-planting never made a good first impression.

Second impression.

Whatever. It'd been eight years.

Finn held open the door as people shuffled through in a steady stream. The lunchtime aromas quickly filled her nose. Bacon, butter, seafood. Yeast from fresh bread and something that smelled deliciously like fresh apple pie. A shiny black-and-white checkerboard floor adorned by a bright red carpet greeted them like celebrities as they were quickly seated in a booth by a window. Nana insisted Maggie sit next to her, so she slid into the booth bench first, completely trapped. There would be no escaping. Finn sat opposite her and Tess sat on the outer edge, warily eyeballing her.

Their waitress, an older woman with a contagious smile and a perfect French braid pinning her hair back, greeted them with a smile and a notepad. Her name tag bore the name Edythe, and Maggie couldn't help but relish in the grandmotherly warmth she radiated.

"Good to see you, Eloise. Glad to know you made it another week," Edythe said, winking.

"You didn't call last week. Thought I'd be tossing the dirt on your coffin by now."

Maggie raised an eyebrow at Finn when both of the women laughed, their smiles captivating the space.

"They're old childhood friends," he replied, half smiling. "They give each other more shit than Tess and I do."

"Well, I have a reason not to die now, Edythe. My grandson here done found himself a fiancée. Isn't she a pretty little thing?" Eloise elbowed Maggie in the ribs. "Just think of all the cute little babies they're going to make. It'll be nice to have those red genes back in the family tree."

Maggie lightly covered her cheek, hoping she could hide a bit of her embarrassment.

"Did you hit her over the head with your club and drag her back to your cave, Finn?" Edythe chuckled and clicked her pen. "Never thought we'd see the day you settled down. Not when there's a big blue ocean out there."

"I don't know what she sees in me, but I sure am a lucky man," replied Finn, briefly glancing at Maggie.

Edythe cupped her fingers around her mouth and turned her back to their table. "Hey, everyone! Finn found himself a girl! Make sure you stop by their booth over here and introduce yourself!" she shouted over the hum of the crowd. "You hang on to this one, young lady." She pointed the tip of her pen at Maggie, and for a brief moment, she thought the waitress was going to throw it at her, just to drive her words home. "He's quite the catch. There may be plenty of fish in the sea, but *this* is the one you want. Don't throw him back. Now, who wants to hear the specials?"

Finn ordered a club sandwich, Eloise ordered chowder, and Tess ordered the special—something having to do with crab, lobster, and cake. She ordered water and the house salad, with light dressing on the side. Edythe told them she'd be back with their drinks in a moment. Just like that, she was with her "extended family". Irrational thoughts swarmed through her head. It was strange, sitting at the table with her husband, sister-in-law, and their grandmother. And a huge secret. Could they tell she was lying? Faking it? And she couldn't keep a secret to save her life.

Maggie arranged her silverware and napkin on the table in front of her, making room for the meal that would probably never be eaten because she knew she was going to die before it ever arrived. Strangers walked by the booth, introducing themselves with names she wouldn't remember in an accent she couldn't understand. They told her how they knew Finn and welcomed her to town.

There was Lucy, who owned the bookshop in the next town over, and Karen, who told Maggie to stop by her salon to get her ends trimmed because they were looking frizzy. And then there was a young mother named Lexi with two bubbly children who gave her wilting flowers from the grass outside in an adorable gesture of friendship.

The stories and the people were overwhelmingly sweet. Maggie smiled but regretted she didn't know any of the stories they shared with her, or those who were involved. And for a reason she couldn't recall, sadness crept into her heart. Such welcoming people so willing to share their lives with her, only to end up that she'd disappoint them all. Would they look at Finn the same way again after she'd gone?

And to make the situation worse, Tess wouldn't stop staring at her with that sisters-know-everything glare. She was beginning to wonder if she had something stuck to her face and shifted in her seat. *Oh God, she'd made eye contact with Tess.*

"So Michelle. I mean, Maggie... What made you drive all the way up here? Finn seemed wicked surprised to see you at the shop."

"Come on, Tess," groaned Finn.

"No, I want to know. *New York* is a long drive for a pop-in visit."

"It's okay," she said. "Well, I had a few days off, and seeing how Finn always makes the drive to come and see me, I thought I would surprise him and return the gesture for once." *Lie, Maggie, lie.*

Tess nodded, and Maggie hoped it was convincing enough to halt the investigation.

"Finn's referred to you as Michelle for months now. Why's that?"

Had she just been caught? No, his sister was merely curious. And smart. Tess knew it wasn't adding up, and rightly so. The entire situation was just weird. "Funny story, actually."

"I'd love to hear it," said Tess.

"Well—" Finn began, but Maggie cut him off.

"It's all right, sweetie pie, I can answer this one." She cleared her throat and glanced across the table at Finn, who fidgeted in his seat. "See, when we first started chatting, I gave him a fake name. In my defense, I had no idea if he was a serial killer or some fat, bald guy hiding behind a fake picture. I didn't even know if anything was even going to come of it, and later I had to fess up to the fake name after he'd been calling me Michelle the entire time. You can never be too careful these days. Now it's just this big inside joke he apparently shared unknowingly with his entire family and is never going to live down." She leaned over the table closer to Tess and cringed. "I'm a bit embarrassed, actually."

In actuality, they had bumped into each other—quite literally—at the slots, and he'd spilled his drink down the front of her sundress. She'd been pissed until Finn grabbed the drink from her hand and poured it down the front of his jeans so they would match. Maggie laughed, Finn smiled... and she'd fallen. Hard. But she doubted anyone wanted to hear *that* story.

The table was awkwardly quiet. Finn looked impressed. Tess looked confused, and Nana studied the dessert menu, completely ignoring the ongoing conversation.

"What do you do?" Tess continued.

"Charity function coordinator," she answered.

"That's a real job?"

"It is to me."

"Do you hunt? Fish? Go mudding?" Tess sat back against the booth, crossing her arms.

All things Finn enjoyed, Maggie presumed. "I'm a vegetarian, and I don't like touching slimy things, but I'm not against getting dirty."

Tess raised an eyebrow. "How did my brother propose?"

Oh, it was on.

"He didn't." Maggie glanced at Finn briefly, and a look of horror glassed over his eyes. Her mouth turned up in a devilish grin. "I did."

Edythe arrived with their drinks. "Tess, leave the girl alone," she said, placing a glass of ice water in front of Maggie. "She's obviously The One, or she wouldn't be here."

"Thank you, Edythe." Maggie may have won that round,

but she wondered what would be next. Hopefully, it wouldn't be a pissing contest while fishing, covered in mud.

Tess took a sip of her drink, then sighed. "Sorry. I'm just a bit protective. As you probably can tell, this just came out of nowhere for us."

"For me, too," agreed Maggie, hoping that would be the end of it.

Lunch passed quickly, and the meal hadn't been as uncomfortable as she expected it to be once she allowed herself to lower her guard. The conversation flowed, mostly with Eloise. It was as if they were old friends catching up on years of absence. Maggie told her about the various charities she raised money for, about her parents—and most of what she told her was true. She didn't need to lie about that. What surprised her the most was how pleasant it was. Finn leaned his elbows on the table, resting his head in his hands, listening. He seemed...content. Relaxed.

Even the conversation with guarded Tess had been pleasant. They had a few things in common—the love for all things horse for one—and sharing that small bond had Tess chuckling and telling barn horror stories over dessert.

When Edythe brought the bill, Maggie swiped it from Finn's grasp. "This one's on me," she told him, handing Edythe back the slip with her credit card. "My treat."

Eloise and Tess thanked her, gathering their belongings while waiting for Edythe to return. Finn stretched his arms above his head, accompanied by a drawn-out yawn. A happy trail of dark hair peeked out at her from beneath his shirt with a teasing *How do you do,* and Maggie looked away. This girlfriend thing was going to be harder than she'd thought.

"Here you go, dear." Edythe placed the billfold on the table with a pen and wiped her hands on her apron. "It was a pleasure meeting you, and I'm sure I will see you around soon. It's a small town, after all. Don't be a stranger."

"It was so nice meeting you, too, Edythe." Maggie signed the credit slip, left her a generous tip, then retrieved her purse from the bench seat.

Eloise slipped her hand around Maggie's forearm, giving it a small pat. "Thank you for the lunch, Maggie. Is it Margaret? I do love a strong traditional name. I hope you'll consider family names for the children. And I do hope you start right away. The longer you wait, the harder it will be to conceive. You don't even need to wait for marriage these days. It's all the rage."

"Nana." Finn chimed in. "Let's take it one day at a time, okay?" he said, following the women to the front exit. "She's been here for like an hour and she's already been interrogated, told what to name her unborn children, and had her job questioned."

Eloise let out a boisterous laugh. "Sometimes, Finnegan, a day is all you've got."

Nana was spot-on.

Chapter Four

Nana's words echoed in Finn's ears. *A day is all you've got.*

Never had something rung truer. Maggie was here. In his sleepy little town. She'd filled his shop with a new breath of fresh ocean air the moment she'd walked through his door. Something had sparked inside him. A light he'd long since extinguished.

And she was single. She could be his. For real this time.

An opportunity presented itself, full and bold, and he'd be a fool to not hook onto it and reel it in. Sitting there in the diner, watching Maggie glow, his heart stirred. He'd be the first to admit, his Nana and sister could be more than overbearing at times, but Maggie had taken them on like a professional. Listening to her interact with them, fully immersed in her stories… It all felt right.

Now here he was, following Nana and Maggie, pushing a shopping cart around the grocery store while they walked arm in arm busting out in fits of giggles. He didn't want the laughter to end.

But it would. This was temporary.

She lived in a different world, and their paths were never destined to cross. She was West, he was East. He was salt, she was sugar. He was dirt and earth and wind and water, and she was light and laughter, glitz and glamour, and she sparkled in the spotlight just like that enormous rock she sported on her finger. That was a life he could never give her. What could he ever offer to make her choose him over that? And in just a few days' time? He needed a plan, and fast.

His chest tightened, and he paused for a moment to catch his breath while the women approached the bakery counter, pointing at fruit-topped pastries and gushing over chocolate ganache. He needed to make Maggie see, show her how wondrous life in Rockport could be, with *him*.

Thoughts and ideas of things he wanted to show her crashed about in his mind. The mussel flats he used to play on during low tides at the beach, and how you could find small pearls inside them. How beautiful sunset was on summer nights. Friday night football and the Lobster Festival that came to town every August, complete with parade and beauty pageant. Small-town life might be slower, but it was beautiful and it was home.

She'd see.

He'd show her home.

Operation: Win Back the Bride had just begun, and it started with prying Maggie away from Nana. She was a witty one with good intentions and a loving heart, but if he let her keep up her antics at this pace, Maggie would be on the first flight out by nightfall. Half the time, even *he* couldn't tell if Nana was being truthful or was up to something, and by the way she was eyeing the baker behind the counter, he'd wager she already had something up her sleeve.

He edged the shopping cart closer to eavesdrop on the conversation.

"Ken is the best baker in the Bay area. Your vision

will be a masterpiece when he's done with it." Nana lightly pushed Maggie front and center. "Ken, this is Maggie and she's marrying my Finn. I'm seeing a summer wedding... rustic...white."

"Well, I'd be happy to whip something up for you." Ken smiled and nodded at Maggie while handing a pie box over the counter to Nana. "Three tiers, fresh flowers, none of those fondant monstrosities. Maybe a surprise custard filling that will just wow the socks off your guests. I can see it, Ellie. I get you." He pointed two fingers at his eyes and then back at Nana.

"Thank you, Ken. Oh! We need to go see Angie, the florist. How do you feel about peonies?" Nana whisked Maggie from the bakery, venturing deeper into the aisles. "Finn, are you coming?"

He sighed. This shit needed to be shut down. "Nana, light of my life"—he took her hands in his—"why don't you go grab your groceries? Maggie and I will get something for dinner, and we'll meet you up front at the register. Tess is waiting in the Jeep, remember."

"Oh yes, that's right. We can talk about the wedding later." She scooted off down an aisle toward the dairy section.

"I'm sorry about Nana. She's excited." A tightness crept along his spine, settling in his neck.

"No, don't be! I think it's kind of cute." Maggie adjusted her purse and glanced at the shoppers passing by. "I feel really bad about disappointing her, though."

"She'll get over it." They stopped in front of an endcap filled with junk food perfect for a stay-in movie night. "So, what do you want for food?" he asked, tossing a bag of salt and vinegar chips into the cart. A movie night sounded awesome. Scary movies meant covering eyes and cuddling close under the stars. He had a projector in the barn somewhere. He could do a movie night. Two more bags of chips found their way into the cart.

"Oh, I'm not too picky," she replied, casually picking up one of the bags of chips, scanning the ingredients, then placing it neatly back on the shelf. "This looks good," she said, picking up a prepackaged veggie kabob from the center section cooler opposite the endcap of junk.

He side-eyed the questionable-looking green *things* she held up for inspection like one of those game show prize presenters. "Moose steak with a side of…whatever that is on a stick?"

She crinkled her nose.

"Pasta it is." Finn turned toward the dairy section, thinking he should probably grab some of the real pasta instead of the dry boxed stuff back in aisle three. There was just something about reconstituted plant matter substitute that didn't sound all that appealing. He spotted Nana covertly spying on him near the bread section and turned toward Maggie. "Would you like to go out for dinner? I know a great little place. Quiet. Vegetarian options," he blurted. One-on-one time, face-to-face, in a nice little place in town might just be the reconnect they needed.

"I'd rather just eat and go to bed, if that's okay. My flight was brutal, and tomorrow is going to be a really rushed day for me. I'm hoping we can get this taken care of and I can catch a red-eye out."

Ouch. She brushed him off, the fruit smoothie in her hand being of more interest than going out. She dropped it into the shopping basket next to the sour gummy worms. He grabbed a package of pumpkin ravioli—that seemed fancy— some organic sauce with a name he couldn't pronounce and shredded parmesan while Maggie engrossed herself in the label of something called Super Green.

"Hey, my brothah!"

Finn immediately recognized the greeting from his

friend, Holokai, a monstrous bear of a man, who could play a ukulele like it was nobody's business. "Kai, good to see you, how you been?" They shook hands in greeting.

"Can't complain. Life is good. Have the bumper sticker to prove it. I saw your grandma over by the cheese. She says you gettin' married for real, bro? Mahalo!"

A panic built inside him. "Dude." Finn tugged at the hair on his nape, unsure as to how to tell his friend about Maggie, especially seeing as Kai had been at their Vegas wedding. He angled his body, opening up the view of the redheaded beauty perusing his junk-food-laden shopping cart.

An audible gasp released from Holokai's mouth. "*Duuude.*"

Finn nodded. "*Dude.*"

"Is that the girl from Vegas? What's she doin' here?"

"It's a long story, man, but the condensed soup version? We're still married."

Kai gritted his teeth, scrunching his nose. "What do we think of that? Do we want to still be married? She still your girl?"

"I want her to be. I just... We haven't spoken in eight years. She showed up at my shop this afternoon, and it all went to hell. My Nana thinks she's my fiancée. She's really here for a divorce." His palms were sweaty. Did the store turn the heat on or something? His secret could slip at any moment. "Don't say *anything*, man. No one knows."

"I feel you." Kai nodded. "Your secret is safe with me." He hesitated. "So this is a good thing?"

"What I wouldn't give for a do-over, man." He watched Maggie from the corner of his eye, slyly replacing his junk food with pieces of fruit and healthier stuff she'd have to force him to eat, and smiled. It was adorable, watching her flitter about the store handing off his Pringles cans to passing employees. "I need to convince her to...*stay.*"

"Then woo her."

Finn eyed his friend.

"Not *woohoo* her..." he said, giving a small pelvic thrust. "*Woo* her. Remind her of why she married you in the first place. Not because of the dare, but of what she saw in you. Hey, think of it like this. You're already one step ahead of every other guy out there. You're already married. Now you just need to show her why you should stay that way. You convinced this island boy to try out a new ocean. You can with her, too."

Maggie's gaze caught his, and she grinned. She recognized Kai. She was walking toward them. Oh God, was he visibly sweating? Where was Nana? He didn't want her anywhere near Maggie in case shenanigans were about to be thrown down.

"I know you." She pointed a finger at Holokai's floral shirt. "Right?" Her eyes widened as if she were suddenly questioning life itself for a brief moment. "Vegas." The word barely escaped on a whisper from those pouty lips.

"How could you forget this face?" Kai framed his cheeks with his palms and grinned.

"What brings you to this side of the ocean?" Maggie asked.

"I wasn't in a good place, and my homeboy here convinced me Maine was just as amazing as the Big Island, and I had to come see for myself. And then I found myself a girl." His eyebrows wiggled fiercely. "She's my ocean now."

"That's so sweet." She smiled genuinely, the sparkle in her eyes captivating his thoughts. "Well, umm..." Maggie paused, glancing around the store.

She was uncomfortable. This had to be awkward for her. "Good seeing you, man," Finn blurted. "I need to go find Nana before she invites the entire store over tomorrow. You still coming?"

"Wouldn't miss it." Kai gave him a light punch to the shoulder, winked at Maggie, and headed off toward produce as Nana veered out into the main aisle.

"I've got my stuff, let's go!" She waved them to follow her as if she were marching into battle and the registers were her intended target. Finn chuckled, found his shopping cart, and blindly followed her to register four.

He let Nana go first, absently placing his items behind the divider on the belt, replaying Kai's words in his mind. He could do this. He could show Maggie he was worthy, and so was his little town. Rockport was a far cry from the city lights, but what it was lacking it made up for in quaint charm and charisma. He just had to show her. And he had only two days. No problem.

He internally cringed, hard.

Finn grabbed the last few items from inside the cart, then looked down at his hands. He held a cucumber and a small container of a cheese dip of some sort, which he didn't remember putting in there. He glanced at the moving belt. He didn't remember putting any of that in the cart, in fact. Where was his beef jerky? And sour gummy worms? "Where's all my stuff?" He turned toward Maggie.

She looked him dead in the eyes and calmly stated, "I have no idea what you're talking about," as she placed a vegetable wrap on the conveyor, staring him down.

His mouth twitched briefly. Game. On.

Chapter Five

The drive back to Garrity Boatworks was pretty enough, but cold. Maggie's California blood wasn't thick enough for the damp chill settling in her bones. She managed to keep her hair in check and her eyes open for most of it, but what she wouldn't give for a jacket. She spied quaint coffee shops and unique stores she wanted to visit, along with an absolutely stunning little touristy park along the edge of the ocean she had to see before she left for California.

Which needed to be soon.

All this talk about babies and family had her ovaries running for the hills. Beverly Hills. Ugh, she wanted to go home. She didn't want kids, and she didn't want to be here. She was no Betty Homemaker. She had her job, her own life, her plans. Which did not include some Podunk town in Maine.

Running into Finn's friend from Vegas had to have been the biggest coincidence yet. Just her luck she'd actually see someone she'd met before, on the opposite side of the country. Just one more person who knew who she truly was.

That could get her in trouble. The last thing she wanted was her network in California finding out about this. Previously engaged while still married, hiding out in Maine with her hottie husband, trying to quietly file for a divorce from the guy she didn't even know she was still married to up until a few days ago. Scandalous.

Considering she had no divorce papers in hand, a call to her father's lawyer was overdue. She should've heard from *someone* by now. She needed answers. Dates. A timeline.

Finality.

Finn parked his Jeep next to Tess's truck and cut the engine. He helped Nana down, gave her a hug, and kissed her on the top of the head.

"I'll see you tomorrow night," he told her.

"You'd better bring that sweet little lady of yours. I'm sure your father is going to want to meet her."

"I'll drag her kicking and screaming."

"Maggie, dear, where are you staying?" Eloise asked from the cab of Tess's truck.

She slid to the ground from the back of the Jeep. "I saw a cute little B & B off the main street on my way here. I thought I might get a room there."

"Nonsense. You'll stay with Finn. I may be old, but I'm no prude. Finn, make her cancel those reservations. She's family. She'll stay with family. You don't get enough time together as it is, and a healthy relationship needs lots of sex."

"*Okay*, Nana." Finn closed the truck door and addressed his sister. "I'll see you at Dad's tomorrow. What time's dinner?"

"Dinner's at five. Game's at six." Tess climbed up into the cab, and then the truck disappeared down the drive.

It was only when the cloud of dust settled that Maggie realized her excuses for avoiding Finn were gone, and sooner or later they would have to get down to business.

Divorce business.

She'd held up her end of the deal and played along. Lunch was nice pretending to be someone she wasn't, and, entertaining as it was, she was in the middle of Nowhere, Maine for a reason. To fix the mess she'd made.

Finn ran his palms over his cheeks and exhaled. "I'm sorry about Nana. She's always told it like it is, even if it's completely inappropriate."

"It's okay, really. I like her. She's adorable. It's refreshing, actually."

"Well, she's going to lose her shit if she finds out you're staying in town, so I guess my place it is. It's probably not what you're used to, but it has a spare room. I still have some work to do here, but I can give you the key." He fumbled with his key ring for a moment. "You know what, screw it. You can follow me in that little toy car of yours. Let's get out of here. I'm sure you have plenty to do."

"Thank you. I'm sure I'll be out of your hair by tomorrow."

"Sure," he said, his voice soft. He turned from her.

"Finn?" she called out after him.

He stopped mid-step. "Yeah?"

"Thank you," she told him, "for being cool about this. I'm really very sorry this has happened. I want to make it up to you."

He let out something close to a grunt and climbed into his Jeep, and Maggie had to hurry to her car to catch up with him before he left her standing there alone.

They traveled through town and toward an array of mountains covered in a luscious green. After turning off the paved road, he led the way over a wooden bridge crossing a small stream and through a thicket that opened up into a grassy field butting up against the edge of a lake. An old barn stood firm in the center of the property. Chipped red paint clung to the wide clapboards among crooked black shutters framing wide windows.

A very quaint, spacious piece of property, but the one thing it was lacking was a house. It took her a moment to grasp that the barn *was* the house.

Oh God, please don't let the spare bedroom be a stall.

Slowly exiting the car, she stared at the monstrous building in front of her. Birds happily chirped and a light breeze swirled through the trees. The earth was alive around her. No screaming pedestrians, no overcrowded roads. No smog. No one questioning her every move. No cameras, no public eye. She had to admit, it was a bit unnerving. And liberating.

"Welcome to our home." His mouth curled up on one side. An attempt at a cruel joke or making light of the situation, Maggie couldn't tell.

Either way, she didn't find it funny. Well, it was a little bit funny. "You live in a barn."

"At least it's not a pigsty. It took me three years and a boatload of money to convert, but I like it." He grabbed her bag from the back seat of her rental and carried it and their groceries effortlessly. "It's even got a workshop out back so I can bring work home with me." He laughed.

"That's dedication." Wooden steps led up to a second-story deck. Maggie ran her hand along the intricate carvings of Celtic knots and spirals on the handrail as she climbed the stairs behind him. "Did you do this?" she asked, tracing the lines with her finger at the top of the railing.

"By hand."

"It's gorgeous," said Maggie. "You have a real talent."

He unlocked the door. "Thank you. I know it's nothing compared to a penthouse in California, but—"

"Finn, it's fine. Seriously." She entered the house. Then stopped in wonderment to stare. It was more than fine. It was absolutely breathtaking. He'd left the beams of the barn intact and exposed the roof. The wall facing the lake had been replaced with wall-to-wall two-story windows. The second floor followed the perimeter of the structure, contained only by a railing made of tree branches, bark still adorning the round lengths. Below her, the open-plan first floor sported a massive kitchen and a living room with a large stone fireplace.

The decor was clean and simple—a bit of the ocean meshed with a dash of his Irish heritage. Light blues and greens met the sand-colored wood, crisp white paired with driftwood accents, and there was hardwood throughout. Windows everywhere. She'd never seen a brighter and more inviting space. "I could fit my entire condo in here. And my neighbor's."

"I'll show you your room," he said, placing the grocery bags on the kitchen table. He led her through a small sitting area and up to the second-floor balcony, where three closed doors lined the wall. "This door is my room—sorry, but I'm not giving that up. This is the bathroom—shake the handle—and the last door is the guest room. You can stay there for as long as you need."

Maggie opened the door. A full-size bed was tucked in a corner with a desk and dresser opposite it. A green and white throw rug covered most of the wooden floor, and thin, sheer curtains waved lazily in the breeze from the open window. "It's lovely, thank you."

Finn set her suitcase down inside the threshold. "I'll leave you to it," he said, then disappeared from view.

She sat on the edge of the bed. "What are you doing, Maggie?" she breathed.

As if in response, her cell phone chimed from her purse, and she jumped to answer it. It was an unknown number to her, but she answered it anyway. "Hello?"

"Good afternoon, is this Margaret Kelley?"

"Yes."

"This is Anna Richards from the law office. I received a

call from your father earlier today. I understand you're in a bit of a predicament?"

Understatement of the year.

"I'll be representing you in court for your divorce from a..." Maggie heard papers flipping in the background. "Finnegan Garrity. Are you in Maine now?"

Lawyer? "Yes. Wait...*court*?"

"Yes, ma'am. Once the documents are filed, we'll schedule a court date to go before the judge to finalize the divorce. Are there any children involved?"

"No, no children. It's uncontested. Can't we just sign and be done with it? How long does it take to see a judge?" She paced the room, trying to make sense of it all.

"Usually a few months."

Months. Not days, months. "That just isn't going to work for me. I need this taken care of like, yesterday."

"I'll see what I can do, Ms. Kelley. I have a colleague who may be able to pull some strings with the judge, but I don't think we're looking at sooner than a month here. County court is pretty busy, even for an uncontested divorce, and there's only one judge. How soon can you both come in and fill out the papers to file? Once we've gotten that out of the way, I'll expedite the court date to finalize."

A quiet panic took root in Maggie's chest. As her legs began to tremble under her, she flopped onto the bed. It creaked under her weight, the sound echoing off the empty walls of the bedroom. "Are you available tomorrow?"

"Well, if you come right after lunch, one o'clock sharp, I can fit you in. I have court tomorrow afternoon."

"Okay." Her voice cracked. Maggie grabbed a pen from her purse and jotted down the information in her planner. She ended the call, then placed the phone down. She stared at the pale yellow wall, attempting to keep her lunch from coming back up. Then she picked up the pillow from the head of the bed, placed it tightly over her face, and screamed. And screamed again.

She drew in a long, deep breath as she attempted to calm herself. Exhaling, she straightened, wiped the moisture from her eyes, and cleared her throat. She was a Kelley. Kelleys could get through anything.

She wouldn't let this little hiccup stop her from doing what she came here to do. Hopefully, the lawyer could make magic happen, and Maggie would be on a red-eye home tomorrow. How would she ever explain this to her father? He expected her to still go through with the wedding once this was all sorted, even though the chance of that happening was sitting solidly at zero.

Winston and she both agreed that marrying each other wasn't what they truly wanted. Finding out she was already married was the excuse—albeit a big one—that they both needed to go their separate ways. She just hadn't had the courage to tell her dad before she'd hopped on the first flight out. Getting the divorce taken care of was still the right thing to do. Maybe Winston would speak with her father and save her from that awkward conversation she dreaded. Two days ago, she'd been applying for a marriage license. And now? She was sleeping in her husband's spare bedroom. Talk about awkward.

"*We don't see applications for a second spouse all that often.*" Maggie singsongingly mocked the words the receptionist had said when the shit had hit the fan at the Los Angeles county clerk's office. Getting married in Vegas had apparently been too easy eight years ago. So much for Vegas. At this point, Elvis had already left the building. Maggie rolled her eyes and groaned, falling backward onto the bed.

Her phone blared her father's number and Maggie contemplated not answering it—he couldn't get mad at her if she didn't answer her phone—but she picked up the phone and swiped the screen to answer it. "Hey," she greeted.

"So?"

Right to the point, as always. "I have good news and bad news. The good news is, I made it here and found him right away. I also spoke to the lawyer, and I'm meeting with her tomorrow to sign the papers."

"That's great news, Margaret. When will you be coming home? People are starting to question where you are."

How could she sugarcoat it? She couldn't. "Here's where the bad news comes in. I have to go to court to get it finalized. The lawyer is going to pull some strings and get me in as soon as possible, but it could take up to a month."

The line was silent.

She knew he was pissed, so she added, "But we're signing the paperwork to get a court date tomorrow afternoon. As soon as he signs, I'll be on the first flight home. I'll come back here to tie up the loose ends at the courthouse, and then this whole nightmare will be over."

"I told the family you're at a friend's wedding for the weekend, so they won't be expecting you until Monday. Are you sure you'll be back by then?"

Four days. Plenty of time. "Absolutely." She even believed it herself. The fiancée ruse would have to be kept up for a bit longer, but it hadn't been all that hard, and if that was what it took to undo this thing, she'd do it. Hell, with a bit of luck, she'd be back on a plane tomorrow night.

"Call me when it's taken care of."

"I'll speak to you soon." She disconnected the call.

The lack of conversation made her uneasy. Maggie groaned and fell backward on the bed. She didn't know what was worse—telling her father or telling Finn.

She was a complete screw-up. How could she do such good work in the world but completely fail at life? She didn't blame Winston. This whole situation fell on her and only her.

She needed to make this right. She sighed. Disappointing

her father was the last thing she wanted to do. He still wanted her to marry Winston, despite what had happened, but she didn't know how to tell him that she no longer wanted to. There was no love lost there. Even their first date had been arranged. She'd gone along with it because she'd needed Winston at the time. He provided her with great opportunity, and starting her charity wasn't something she could do alone. Her lifelong dream of building a nonprofit medical wing for underprivileged children fighting cancer could happen because of him. He carried a prominent name and was a sought-after plastic surgeon. With his name backing her, there would be no stopping her. Their arrangement worked well. She was able to use his clout, and he got the arm-candy wife whose daddy had the money. Who needed love, right?

Maggie rubbed her brow with shaky fingers. Winston was gone. They were no longer together, and what was done was done. The end. Final. *For better or worse* turned out to be *run at the first sign of trouble*. She leaned back against the headboard and sighed. Why did she even bother? He didn't want her, and he'd made that crystal clear. The breakup had been amicable, sort of…after the fight of the century. So why was she still wasting her thoughts on him?

A twinge of guilt manifested its way into Maggie's conscience. It was hard to let go of dreams. All those children waiting for her. She'd been fighting for this for the past six years. It hurt to know she'd be disappointing so many people, and she took it to heart. She'd poured her soul into her life's work of helping others. And now, just like that, it was gone. All of it. Because of one stupid mistake she'd made on her twenty-first birthday. The first rebellious act of her life had changed everything. Maggie would be the first to admit she hadn't been the most responsible adult during her trip to Vegas, but it had been her first time away from home on her own. The freedom had been…liberating.

No. There had to be another way. She refused to give up on it. This was her *dream*, and she'd be damned if she was going to let some jerk like Winston take that from her. She would find a way to make it happen. She hadn't quite figured it out, but as soon as she could get back to California, she'd be in touch with every contact she had and get it done.

Maggie unfurled herself from the bed and ventured out into the hallway. "Finn?" she called, drawing out his name. "I have something to tell you!"

He stepped out from the bathroom and into the hall, followed by a cloud of steam.

Shirtless.

Damp and glistening like some teen vampire.

Staring at her. Smoldering, even.

Mere feet stood between her and washboard abs. His cargo shorts hung loosely around the vee of his hips, leaving what lay beneath to her very vivid imagination. She faced those abs. And that vee, the one disappearing beneath the waistband of his shorts in perfect symmetry. The one that made smart girls stupid.

"Hey, my eyes are up here." He circled a finger around his face.

Tomorrow couldn't come soon enough. Her glance met his. "I spoke to the lawyer."

"I figured. So... You're a screamer, huh?" He used the towel clutched in his hand to dry his dripping hair.

Stray droplets sprayed from his hair in all directions while she contemplated if the sexual innuendo was him being serious or just him trying to get under her skin from her scream in the spare bedroom earlier. Probably a bit of both. "You would know," she muttered.

He raised an eyebrow. "I've got all night to jog my memory."

She ignored the insinuation. "That's great, because we

need to talk." She started for the stairs to the first floor. "First, I want to thank you for being so accommodating and nice. You didn't have to be. Second, we have an appointment tomorrow with the lawyer to sign the papers. It's at one."

"So that's it, then? Just sign and done?"

Maggie hopped lightly off the bottom step to saunter over to the nearest couch. She plopped herself down on the plush cushions. "Unfortunately, no. We have to wait for a court date and go before a judge to get it finalized. It's going to take a month, at least. That is, if the lawyer can pull some strings."

"So you're going to be staying here for a month?" He seemed a bit taken aback by her news. Understandable.

"No, I'm going home after we sign. I'll come back for the court appearance. I have a meeting on Monday I absolutely can't miss. My job kind of depends on me being there. It's the first *big* account I've taken on solo. I also have all the things to cancel for the wedding that will never be and damage control to do. My father started planning this big wedding before Winston had even proposed. It could be only during specific weekends due to everyone's schedules." She sighed. "No one ever asked me what *I* wanted for my wedding. No, little Maggie always did what she was told. I don't even know why I'm telling you all this."

Finn rubbed his forehead with his fingertips, massaging the area over his eyes in tiny circles. "That sounds exhausting."

"You have no idea."

"Do they give deposits back if it turns out the bride is already married?"

She glared at him. "Shut up."

"You *do* realize my grandmother is expecting you tomorrow for dinner, right? It's Friday friends and family fun night."

Oh, sweet Eloise. She'd completely forgotten about not killing Grandma.

Chapter Six

Maggie was going to kill him. Finn gripped the steering wheel until his knuckles turned white. Missing their meeting with the lawyer wasn't how he wanted to pick things back up with her, but he hadn't any other choice. How was he going to explain this?

He sighed and turned the key. As the Jeep roared to life, he glanced at the time. He was *late* late. Even if he sped the entire way from his dad's house, he'd never make it downtown in time to possibly catch her. Finn grabbed his phone from the cup holder and swiped the screen on.

He growled, banging his head back against the headrest. He'd never gotten her number. Why hadn't he asked for her number? Wasn't that the first thing guys did when trying to pick up women? Admittedly, it had been a while since he'd played the dating game, but come on. He quickly Googled the number for the lawyer's office and hit the call button. It rang.

And rang.

"Come on, answer," he breathed. An answering machine

beeped back at him. *Dammit.*

He put the Jeep in gear and headed up the drive. Maggie would be sympathetic, right? He understood they'd made plans, but family came first. She would get that. Yeah, she'd be all *redheaded* angry at him, but there was still time. He would set the appointment himself. Everything would work out, and they'd be okay. There was some sort of hiccup in the universe that had brought them back together again, and he wasn't about to let that slip past him, because he had a real chance at happiness.

Boats, and the water, had always been his life. If it had to do with working on a boat, being in a boat, or on the water, that was his happiness in life. But as much as he loved it, nothing compared to what he could find with Maggie. She made his heart leap just as much as the tides did.

He'd thrown himself into his work so much he'd never really put a lot of thought into taking on a relationship. Especially not after what he'd seen his sister go through with Colin's sperm donor. This wasn't the first time he'd had to stop what he was doing and rush over to the house. He had vowed a long time ago that, if he ever got the chance to be blessed with a family of his own, he'd never be *that* man.

• • •

Maggie paced the sidewalk in front of the lawyer's office. She was a half hour early, just in case, and had even brought Finn a coffee, which she was now drinking because she'd finished hers already. She glanced at the time on her phone. One twenty.

He was late.

He'd left for work early, she supposed, as he wasn't around when her alarm of seven a.m. blared, and she hadn't had a chance to remind him of their one o'clock appointment.

But she was pretty sure it was something he wouldn't have forgotten. Filing for divorce after an eight-year marriage you didn't realize you were still in wasn't exactly a when-I-get-around-to-it kind of thing. The office was a central meeting point between his job and the house, according to her phone's GPS, so it made sense to meet up.

So much for that.

A door creaked open behind her and Maggie turned toward it.

"I'm so sorry, Ms. Kelley, but I must be going. I'm already late."

Maggie forced a weak grin. "I understand. I don't know what happened. He said he'd be here." She'd even waited outside for him as a beacon, in case he couldn't find the place.

Anna gave Maggie's shoulder a squeeze. "If you want to sign and leave them with my receptionist, you're welcome to."

"No, no, that's okay. I need to see him actually sign the paper. I need to know this is *done*. We don't have that great of a success rate for signing important papers at the moment."

"I understand. Give my office a call on Tuesday and we'll try again."

Maggie fought back frustrated tears. Tuesday. "Any chance you take weekend clients? I can pay you."

"I'm so sorry. I'll be out of town this weekend, and I will be in court all day Monday. Come see me first thing Tuesday, and we'll get this taken care of."

Maggie waited until the lawyer got in her car and drove away before stomping her feelings into the pavement.

What was she supposed to do now? She looked at her phone, only to shove it in her bag. Then she pulled it back out. She didn't have his phone number, so she tried the one she had for the shop. No answer.

Blood pulsed in her ears. Her chest tightened and she fought for a full breath. A wave of nausea swept over her while her heart felt like it was going to claw its way out of her chest. If there was ever an appropriate time for a full-blown panic attack, her current situation certainly applied. She opened the car door and slipped into the driver's seat. Gripping the steering wheel with both hands, she sat there for a moment, hoping she could calm herself enough to drive back to Finn's lake house.

She took a quick mental inventory of her daily planner. Charity board meeting Monday afternoon. Gala walk-through for the Van Holden account Tuesday evening. The *L.A. Times* was expecting her and her assistant, Cara, on Wednesday morning to finalize the contract for the Women of the Times fundraiser. She'd worked her ass off for that account. They were taking a leap of faith entrusting it to her. Two full pages. *Oh God…*

Finn may have helped flush her career down the toilet.

Word of her unreliable behavior would have the social syndicates buzzing. She'd be fired. Or worse…*blacklisted*. She'd never be commissioned to host another event again. Maggie would be the talk of the town. She could see the headlines now: *Senator's Son Engaged to Married Woman.* They'd probably give her a two-page spread for *that*.

Finn needed to sign those papers.

The lawyer's words still rang fresh in her ears. *Call on Tuesday.* So much for catching a red-eye.

She had damage control to do. And phone calls to make. She started the engine and backed out of the parking spot.

There were so many ways she planned to murder him. Verbally, of course. He deserved a hell of a good tongue-lashing after the stunt he'd pulled today. What could have been more important than their divorce?

Maybe his Jeep didn't start, and because they stupidly hadn't exchanged numbers, he couldn't call to let her know he'd be late. But he could have called someone for a ride. Or called the lawyer. Maybe he'd just lost track of time. Got lost. Gone to the wrong office.

What if there had been an emergency? That could explain why he'd stood her up. His workshop went up in flames. He was involved in a hit-and-run. What if he'd told his family the truth, and his grandmother had died from the shock of it all? So many plausible reasons, and she felt guilty for even being angry with him, even though most of her reasoning was far-fetched. There had to be a sensible answer.

Her first stop after the lawyer's office was his workshop. The CLOSED sign still hung in the uncharred window. The second stop was his house. She pulled the car to a stop in the driveway, his Jeep absent. He wasn't home. She hadn't locked the door when she'd left—and she'd felt terrible for not doing so—but Finn had never mentioned giving her a key.

There was nothing else to do but wait.

The house was quiet when she entered. Peaceful. Something rare and elusive to her—she didn't remember the last time she was able to sit with her thoughts. The welcome silence was short-lived, however, as she had very important phone calls to make. Her first call was to Cara, whom she had to lie to. As much as she adored the woman, she had a big mouth.

Cara huffed and puffed when Maggie told her she'd have to go to the Monday morning meeting in her stead, but she reluctantly agreed. It absolutely killed Maggie to hand over the reins, but it had to be done. The show must go on—with or without her. If she could drag Finn into Oceanside Legal first thing Tuesday morning, she could be home in time for the Van Holden gala walk-through. And all would be well.

She placed her phone on the end table beside the couch and sat down, sinking into the leather cushions. She slipped out of her heels and curled into the corner of the couch, staring at the exposed beam ceiling for a moment before closing her eyes. She needed peace. She needed the calm before the storm.

• • •

Something touched her shoulder, nudging her slightly. Her eyes flew open. Finn stared down at her, and Maggie groaned. Had she really fallen asleep? She shot upright on the couch. "Where have you been?"

"I have a job," he replied, eyes narrowing. He fell into the couch beside her, his frame encompassing much of the space.

Maggie drew her knees up beside her to escape his collapse. "I went there. I was counting on you today."

He let his head relax on the back of the couch and let out a long sigh. "I know."

"You stood me up."

"There was something I had to take care of."

"Something more important than signing my divorce intent papers? I told you the time we were supposed to meet the lawyer. I said I had to fly back to L.A."

"You said Monday."

"Yeah, because I have a job, too, Finn," she spat. "Quite a few important ones. I *have* to be back in Los Angeles no later than Monday morning. And now, because you didn't feel like showing up or sticking to our bargain, we can't get another appointment until *Tuesday*. Do you realize how much you've screwed me over? Like, seriously, my entire career is in jeopardy right now." She rose from the couch, clenching her fists at her sides. She wasn't a fighter, but damn, she felt like punching something. "I work for some very high-profile clients. Very rich and influential people. If word got out that I was here... If they thought I flaked out on them—because there's no way I could *ever* tell the truth about us, it would destroy—I'd never work again."

"I'm sorry, but—"

She whipped around to face him. "No, you're not. You made a conscious decision to leave me standing there waiting like an idiot. What happened to our deal? I pretend to be this mysterious girlfriend no one has ever met for a day, and you would sign the papers. Well, Finn, I went above and beyond girlfriend to fiancée." She crossed her arms and continued pacing. Unbelievable. She should have driven to pick up his behind instead of foolishly agreeing to meet him at the office. Her mistake… She thought he would show up. Like her daddy had told her countless times before, *don't count on anyone but yourself to do something right.*

He glanced at the cell phone in his hand, then back at her. He swallowed hard, as if he had so much to say, but kept his thoughts to himself. He slipped the phone into his pocket.

If that's how he wanted to be, then fine. She'd continue. "Is there somewhere else you need to be?"

"Maggie, look." A long breath left his lips. "I'm sorry, I really am. But there was just something else I had to deal with."

She threw her hands up in exasperation. "What?"

His expression told her he struggled with answering the question. "Making sure my sister's ex didn't beat the crap out of her again. My dad called and I had to go. There's no one else at the house who can deal with that asshole when he drinks."

Maggie's jaw opened slightly before she clamped it shut. Feeling like the biggest jerk in the world didn't begin to encompass how awful she felt for blowing up at him. "I'm sorry. I didn't know." She began to pace, because that's what awkward situations called for. Pacing, and avoiding eye contact.

He cleared his throat and swallowed hard. "I wouldn't expect you to." His words were remarkably calm. "It's family dinner tonight. They're waiting for us." He leaned forward, scrubbing his face with his palms. He dragged them down slowly, exhaling as he pinched the skin between his brows. "Look, I know you're pissed at me right now, and you have every right to be. I should have called the lawyer first thing to let you know I couldn't make it. I could have made better choices, but my mind was on Tess and Colin. I didn't realize after eight years it would be that big of a deal to you to have to wait one more day. I mean, did you ever think about how this has affected me? The world doesn't revolve around you, Maggie. I've been listening to you go on and on for the last ten minutes about how your *job* is so important. Well, my *family* is important to me. Shit happened, I did what I thought was best, and they come first."

She stopped pacing. She hadn't, in fact, given it a second thought. Or a first thought, for that matter. Maggie had thought about nothing but herself from the time she stepped foot in the county clerk's office, hell-bent on marrying Winston. Finn didn't have to make her look like an idiot. She did a great job of that herself.

"What if I was married and with a couple of kids? It's not *unfathomable* for a thirty-three-year-old guy to be settled down. What if I had to tell my wife about some dare I accepted during a drunken booze fest? What if I had to tell the love of my life that our marriage wasn't legal?" He pointed at Maggie. "Getting married was *your* idea. *You're* the one who said you'd take care of it. Done deal. Goodbye. Have a nice life. Well, I've been living the last eight years not even giving it another thought, and then one day you decide to walk in here like you own the place? Demanding I do shit just so you can *maybe* go get married to some hoity-toity rich guy you're not even with anymore. I don't think so." Finn stared at her, one eyebrow half-cocked. Waiting.

"But you're not married," she blurted out.

"I'll wait a minute while you let that one sink in." He leaned back, lacing his palms behind his head.

Keep digging that hole, Maggie. She knew very well he was married.

To her.

Maggie returned to the couch, balancing on the arm. "I'm a selfish brat," she proclaimed.

"There it is."

"Well... Shit happened back there in Vegas eight years ago, and we have to deal with it. My fault, your fault, that doesn't even matter at this point. What matters is we need to make it right, and we need to fix this. Sitting here arguing about the past isn't going to make what we did right."

"Maybe if you could stop thinking about yourself for five minutes you'd notice I'm struggling with this just as much as you are. This isn't your world, Maggie. It's mine. This is my family, my home, and you're in it for merely a fraction of time. Bitch and moan all you want, but it'll get done when it gets done. And that's all there is to it."

She slid off the couch arm, landing on the cushion with a slight bounce. At twenty-one, she had been a crazy, thrill-seeking, newly legal daredevil who didn't realize her actions could have repercussions. And Finn had been the horny bastard who'd followed through with it. It was water under the bridge. He was right about that. This wasn't an argument she was going to win. As much as it pained her to do so, she gritted her teeth and apologized. "I'll work remotely. I'll figure it out. I'm sorry." Now there was a solution. If she was going to be stuck in the middle of nowhere against her will, she'd make the most of it. "God, I need some coffee."

"So are we done?" He groaned while rising from the couch.

Maggie sank deeper into the plush without his weight to counterbalance her own. "If you hadn't noticed, this is my pissed face. I'm brooding." She framed her face with her hands.

"Well, it's going to have to be done for now, because we're wicked late and Tess is blowing up my phone with texts screaming at me. See?" he said, turning his phone so she could see it. "All caps."

"So go."

"I can't go without you. I told my dad you were coming."

"Why would you do that?" she replied, tucking her feet under her. "It's just dinner."

"Well, there *is* baseball."

"I don't do baseball."

"*Michelle* would do baseball," he countered, teasing her.

"*Michelle* doesn't exist. You know, if you've told your family *anything* about this fake girlfriend of yours, you might want to clue in the actress she's being portrayed by."

Finn stretched his arms over his head. His shirt rose with them, exposing that sexy happy trail of hair disappearing under the recognizable elastic of a Calvin Klein waistband. It was nice to see Maine wasn't completely in the dark ages.

"She likes baseball," he nodded with surety.

Maggie grabbed the throw pillow beside her and chucked it at him. It thumped him in the chest, then fell flat to the floor. "No, she doesn't."

"How would you know? You've never met her." He picked up the pillow and scrunched it between his fists.

"Do you talk to a lot of imaginary people?"

"Just the hot ones." He grinned widely and reflexively covered his groin when the second throw pillow headed in his direction. "So are you coming to dinner or not? Nana's going to be there. I would love if she made it to Christmas."

Finn sure knew how a guilt trip worked. "Stop. Your Nana is the epitome of good health for her age." Maggie rolled her eyes. There would be no more sympathy cards played for

Nana. "Fine. I'll go with you to dinner. But I'm not doing baseball." She rose from the couch to pick up her shoes.

"Oh, come on. Where's that adventurous girl? Do I have to *dare* you in order for you to play?" He tossed both pillows back onto the couch.

She headed for the stairs. "I need to change," she told him, ascending to the second floor.

"Ten minutes!" he called out. "We're late!"

"That seems to be a running theme with you," she muttered.

Once reaching her room, Maggie kicked the door closed behind her and tugged her suitcase up onto the bed. She hadn't packed much in the ways of practical outfits, as she hadn't planned on staying for more than the weekend. Most of her things were business attire and not something one would wear to a family dinner. "Business cas" would just be weird while trying to fit in with the country folk. Ocean folk? They certainly weren't city people.

She chose a delicate, flowing, off-the-shoulder blouse, curve-hugging black Dior capris, and her favorite cranberry Louboutin heels that made her calves look sexy as hell in jeans. She touched up her makeup, let down her hair, and ran her fingers through it in a feeble attempt to control her unruly waves, then ventured out to find Finn.

She found him all right, standing in her doorway directly in her path. She stopped short, nearly colliding into his chest.

"Wow," he said softly. "I can't wait to see you play with balls in that."

Maggie slapped his arm. "In your dreams, sweet cheeks."

"Are you ready to go?" he asked, jingling his keys.

"Yes. Is this something your imaginary girlfriend would approve of?" She struck a pose, jutting out her hip to the side.

His eyes flickered, catching a ray of the sunset from the nearby window. "You look really nice."

Deflecting with compliments. Typical male. "I'm still mad at you. But thank you."

Finn cracked a smile as he walked to the front door and held it open for her. "I think playing with some balls might change that. Endorphins and all that."

Maggie rolled her eyes and brushed by Finn while he locked up. "I'm not going to be playing with any balls, baseball-sized or not."

"Oh, come on. You should try it. You might just like it. And want to play with them *a lot*." He took the steps two at a time to catch up.

It was hard to argue with that. It was that same playful taunting that had her doing much more than playing with Finn's figurative balls in Vegas. He knew how to rile her competitive side and use it against her, just like he was doing now. First came the cute little comments, then the frisky double entendres, followed by a lively game of wills where it was she who ultimately gave in and jumped on the sexual tension so thick you could swim in it.

Which absolutely could not happen this time around. Finn and she had had their moment in the sun. And it had long since set. The sooner she was out of here, the better. They weren't friends—they weren't lovers. What they shared boiled down to a clerical error and nothing more.

The evening air hit her hard, and Maggie wrapped her arms around her middle in a feeble attempt to cut the chill. She was stupidly unprepared for the North and shivered at the thought of what it must be like in the dead of winter.

"Here." Finn thrust a hooded sweatshirt at her. "You look like you need it more than I do."

She gripped the faded fabric in her hands for a moment, then slid it on over her head. "Thank you," she replied, looking down at the Boston Red Sox logo emblazoned across her chest. She hiked herself into the passenger seat and buckled up.

The drive to Tess's house was filled with classic rock songs lost to the wind and shouts of broken conversation drowned out by the engine. Although she couldn't decipher a word Finn was saying to her, she smiled and nodded anyway. Keeping up pleasantries was a must if she was going to get through this alive. She could think of a million ways this evening could go, and every single one of them ended in an argument, embarrassment, or a screaming match. Maggie pulled the hoodie closer to her body and that lingering woodsy, manly smell of its owner assaulted her nose. She closed her eyes and sank deeper into its warmth, its security. Sadness briefly settled over her—she longed to know what it was like to feel such safety enveloped by the arms meant to hold her.

She should be on a plane right now drinking champagne out of a real glass etched with the airline logo. Instead, she was heading into God-knows-where with the bad boy from the other side of the tracks. That rough, un-groomed exterior and the tousled-hair-lumberjack thing he had going on were uncharted waters. Ties and cufflinks were her norm, not scruffy beards and backward baseball caps sporting beer logos. Nope. That was slumming it, her mother would say. Against everything her family stood for. Right up there with the Montagues. He was the addiction her upbringing forbade.

As they rounded a corner, Finn slowed and turned left off the pavement and onto a dirt road. The front tire hit a pothole, and the Jeep pitched sharply to the right. Maggie gripped the seat as if her life depended on it. Finn laughed at her and changed the radio station. A twangy country song blared at her. Of course. Because it wasn't country until you turned off the paved road.

A tall iron gate framed each side of the drive. A large sign with HOOVES FOR HEALING scrawled across it towered over them as they drove down the narrow way. White fence lined both sides of the road, following them as they headed closer to the white farmhouse in the distance. A few horses grazed in a pasture nearby. Very picturesque, like something on a gas station postcard. Vehicles were strewn across the front yard—everything from a rusted green tractor to a truck jacked up on three wheels—but still, it looked…nostalgically attractive. "Is this Tess's place?" Maggie asked, slowly loosening her grip as Finn stopped.

"Yeah, she lives here with my dad. We all figured she could use the help once he retired from the boat business." Finn parked his Jeep next in line with several other cars. "She owns an equine therapy business."

Maggie drew in a breath. "Anything I should know ahead of time?"

"Yeah. My family is all kinds of crazy." He winked and cracked a smile, and she had no idea if he was being serious or just trying to get her worked up.

As Maggie slid down from the passenger seat, Tess appeared on the front porch. She held the screen door open with her foot while leaning over the threshold to yell at them, "You're late! I have a ten-pound pig ass on the table waiting for you, so get yourselves in the house!" She disappeared as quickly as she'd appeared, leaving the screen door slamming against its hinges.

Finn started toward the house, but stopped short of the stairs, turning back to look at her. Maggie's feet stood planted firmly to the ground next to the Jeep. Her heart was racing as fast as her head was spinning.

"You okay?" he asked. He was by her side in three steps.

She fanned her face, a feeble attempt at keeping the sweat at bay. "I can't do this," she muttered. There was a reason she'd gone into nonprofit instead of sales—she couldn't look people in the eye and say untruths. "Two people over lunch is one thing, but the whole family? I'm going to screw it up. I'm pretty sure Tess hates me, and I think your Nana knows something's up." God, she was going to *throw up*. "And what about PDA? We're supposed to be engaged. I can't...I— "

"Hey." He lifted her chin with a finger and searched her eyes. "It's going to be fine. Please don't freak out on me."

"I'm a terrible liar, Finn." Releasing a breath through pursed lips did nothing to calm her churning insides. "I shouldn't be here. I shouldn't be doing this."

"What they don't know won't hurt them. It's none of their business anyway. It's ours and ours alone. Let them think what they want to think."

"They're going to think I'm your fiancée. And it's going to break your Nana's heart when I leave here. It's just not right." She could tell the truth, laugh it off, and she wouldn't have to lie anymore.

Something in his eyes spoke the words he would not. A silent plea to help him. An urgency lingered there, framed by remarkably long lashes she'd failed to notice before, and the brush of light freckles splashed over his cheekbones. She fought the sudden urge to run her fingers through his tousled hair and make some sense of order out of it. The ends that curled up behind his ears and around his nape drove her crazy, and she wanted to grab them in her fists and just—

"Hey, you two, I *said* dinner's waiting!" This time, Tess yelled, filled with complete annoyance.

"All right!" Finn shouted back at his sister with the same irritation. Then, waiting until she was gone again, he said, "I'll go first thing and sign the damn papers. Let *me* deal with you leaving. That's on me." He slipped his hand around Maggie's and tugged slightly. "Let's do this."

Ready or not, they were going in.

Chapter Seven

The buzz of conversation and laughter grew louder as Finn led Maggie through a maze of old rooms and hallways. The farmhouse was his childhood home, which his sister and nephew now shared with his father. It was ancestral and charismatic with spurts of modern mushed together with old rustic charm. Framed pictures adorned every nook and cranny with people posed with livestock. Tarnished medals were hung over the corners of some of the frames. The hallway had settled in a decor stalemate, with one half being equine in nature and the other nautical, with his mother being a woman of the earth and his father a man of the sea. A recording of Billie Holiday played softly somewhere in the distance, bringing the pictures from days gone by front and center.

"Is this you?" Maggie traced the figure of a gangly teen wearing a tattered jersey forever frozen in time by dusty glass.

"Oh yeah. That's from the year I got really into the Mighty Ducks movies and hockey, except I didn't have anywhere to play it, so I just pretended I was on the team and carried around a stick wearing rollerblades and acted like I knew what I was doing."

Maggie looked up at him, her mouth curling at one corner. "That's adorable."

"Have you ever tried walking on crushed rock while wearing rollerblades? I don't recommend it." He shrugged. "I don't even know how to play hockey. I bet those girls from middle school still think I do, though."

"That one Bash Brother was pretty hot," she said, flashing him a teasing smile. Maggie took a few steps forward, taking in every picture and painting adorning the walls. That was the story of his life, plastered up there in mismatched frames and faded handwritten titles. Memories he'd forgotten about until just that moment, standing there with her, wanting nothing more than to sit out on the front porch swing in the summer telling her all about the stories behind those memories.

"What about this one?" She pointed to a picture of him standing next to his dad and a wooden fishing boat.

He smiled. "That was the first boat I'd helped my dad build. I was nine. That picture was taken right before the first time we took it out on the water." A laugh erupted from within him and he shook his head slightly at the memory.

"Do you still have it? What a keepsake to keep in the family business."

"Hell no," he replied. "We started taking on water a half mile offshore. Had to get rescued by the Coast Guard. That boat sank to the bottom of the ocean." He stared at the picture for a moment and could almost taste the salt water in his mouth. "That was a great day," he sighed.

"You make me wonder what you consider a bad day." She paused briefly while passing a picture of Tess sitting proudly on top of her prized mare before continuing down the hallway toward the kitchen.

"You ready to go meet my crazies? I think Tess made

cupcakes."

She nodded. "You had me at cupcakes."

A welcoming glow illuminated the far end of the hallway. Laughter bounced off the walls, growing louder as they approached. Maggie tightened her grip on Finn and he squeezed her hand, a small, reassuring gesture he was sure she appreciated as he led her closer to impending doom.

A collective cheer resonated throughout the room as they entered. "They're here!" Tess pushed back her chair and stood, turning her attention to the dishes splayed out on the long farm table. "Dig in, everyone!"

His father rose, placing the cloth napkin he held on the table. "Finn, introduce me to this breathtaking beauty."

Finn guided Maggie to a chair. "Dad, this is Maggie, my *girl*—fiancée. Maggie, my dad, Alastair."

"It's a pleasure to meet you, Mr. Garrity. Thank you for having me." Maggie shook his outstretched hand, then sat. She pulled off the hoodie, slinging it over the back of the dining room chair.

"Maggie? I thought it was Michelle. That's a fine Irish name. You'll fit right in." Alastair shrugged, brushing off the confusion as if it was his mistake. "The pleasure is all mine, young lady. I'm happy you could join us. Now let's eat."

Finn inwardly groaned. This was going to be so much fun. Pitchers of ice water and bottles of wine were passed around the table and glasses filled while Tess fussed over the plates and bowls of food, making sure everyone had enough of everything.

"So who are all these people?" Maggie whispered to Finn while casually trying to stab a chunk of cucumber on her plate with her fork. "I'm trying to keep up, but apparently you all use a different alphabet in the North. These accents are something else."

"Mmm. Yeah," he said, swallowing. "They get worse the

farther north you go. Where are my manners?" He rose from the table. "Everyone, this is Maggie. Maggie, you know Tess, and my dad," he started, going around the table. "That's my nephew, Colin," he told her, pointing to a blond boy barely tall enough to reach the table by himself. "That's my cousin Ryan and his wife, Torry. High school sweethearts with a ton of kids running around here somewhere." The couple waved at the introduction.

"Then there's Nana, her sister, Genny. At the far end down there is my sister's friend, Jo, her boyfriend whose name I don't know"—he chuckled at his own joke—"and those two guys are from my rock-climbing group. Will and John. They're really here only for baseball, but Will has a crush on my sister, so he comes to bother her, too." A collective "ooh" from the guests had Will blushing. Finn returned to his seat. "Some more guys will be showing up for the game. It's a kind of a once-a-month thing for the months it doesn't snow. Keeps us out of trouble. Nana runs a tight ship with these guys. They behave and she gives them cookies."

Maggie waved and said hello to everyone before settling back in her chair to eat. "And what about your mom?" she asked, over the noise of dinner chatter.

There was a lull in the conversation at the same moment she asked, and Finn cleared his throat. "My mother, Moira, passed away from cancer when we were young."

"I'm so sorry, Finn." Her cheeks flushed.

He'd embarrassed her and felt like an ass. "I should have told you." He pushed a piece of meat around his plate.

"Yeah, I could have used a heads-up on that one," she whispered. Maggie placed her fork next to her plate and folded her hands in her lap.

"This is awkward for you. I'm so sorry. I can spill my drink on myself, if it'd help." She chuckled, and he smiled. Referring back to their first encounter got him the reaction he'd hoped for, taking the edge off a bit. His family could be a bit...overwhelming. "Are you not hungry? Can I make you something less meaty? I forgot to tell Tess you're a vegetarian."

"Oh, no thank you. I'm fine. There's plenty for me to eat. While I'm sure Tess is a fantastic cook, I'm just not used to seeing so many...animals chopped up in one sitting. It smells delicious, which makes the mental struggle only that much harder. All I can think of is *Wilbur...Wilbur...Wilbur.* Add to that the humiliation of not knowing my mother-in-law is dead, and most of the table overhearing my stupidity... Some fiancée I am."

Across the table, his father grabbed a bottle of wine, poured a bit into his glass, then raised it. The murmur of voices quieted. "We can't finish this dinner without blessing our newest family member. So without further ado, may love and laughter light your days and warm your heart and home," he recited, his Irish lilt suddenly much thicker with the words. "May good and faithful friends be yours, wherever you may roam. To my family and our friends, and to Finn and my new daughter, Maggie."

A communal Irish *"slàinte"* toast resounded throughout the room, followed by the clinking of glasses, and Maggie looked like she wanted to crawl under the table and hide. She had been in the room for all of two minutes and was already a daughter.

"So," his father continued. "Is she pregnant?" Heads whipped in Finn's direction.

He choked on his drink and pounded on his chest in a feeble attempt to get in a breath, as Maggie's cheeks turned a shade of scarlet. He sputtered, downed the rest of his glass, and then finished Maggie's to subdue his cough. "No, Pop, Maggie's not pregnant." He pushed back his chair. The wooden legs screeched against the floor. "I need another drink."

Maggie slapped his thigh and squeezed. Had her nails been any sharper, they would have drawn blood. His palm found her fingers, urging her to loosen the death grip, just a little. Shots had been fired, and he understood. He wasn't going anywhere.

"We're all thinking it. Your dad is just asking it," someone piped up.

"You haven't brought a girl home in... I don't even remember. When was the last time you dated?" Tess shot him a look over the rim of her glass.

"Does that matter? And since when are you all keeping tabs on my dating life?"

"Oh, come on now," Torry said from the end of the table. "Something is up if a catch like you is still single at your age."

Finn's jaw slackened. "At my age?" What was going on?

"You've been in that shop for months, and all of a sudden you're bringing a girl home, and she's your fiancée to boot? Something's up." His father leaned on the table, his elbow resting on the edge slightly.

"*Dad.* Maggie is *not* pregnant."

"Definitely not pregnant," Maggie reiterated.

Finn took a bite. "Why is it so hard for you guys to believe there may be things I don't want to share with everyone? Like my love life."

The table was silent for a moment, then they burst out in laughter. "What else is there to talk about?" Nana chimed in.

"For shame, Nana, for shame," Finn shot back. "Grandpa would have my back."

Finn sat back in his chair, folding his arms behind his head. "Is this what you guys do all day when I'm not around? Talk about me behind my back?"

Tess stood briefly to grab a dinner roll. She took a large bite and in between swallows, she nodded and told him calmly, "We have spreadsheets."

"Oh, I love spreadsheets," Maggie replied.

Finn's mouth went slack and he stared at her. "Don't let them get to you."

"She fits right in!"

"What's a spreadsheet?" chirped a small-voiced Colin from the corner. "I want one, too!"

Finn was happy for the interruption. This was exactly why he'd made up his fake girlfriend Michelle in the first place, so that he wouldn't be the one getting grilled at dinner.

"Well then. Here's to many babies to coddle after the wedding." His father raised his glass and took a swig, then grinned widely. "Now that the elephant has left the room, tell me about yourself. What do you do, Maggie? Finn hasn't told us a damn thing about you."

"I run a charitable event and fundraising firm."

Alastair's eyes narrowed. "And what does that mean, exactly?"

"Well," she said, straightening in her chair, "when national charities or nonprofits need help raising funds for things like hospitals or say…children's cancer research, they come to me. I find donors, sponsors, and organize events like galas and swanky dinners to raise that money when they wouldn't necessarily be able to do it on their own. I have a full networking and marketing team at my disposal who run in some pretty influential circles, so we do fairly well."

Alastair nodded, as if he was adding all of her credentials to some mental checklist. "And your parents?"

"My father is a cardiothoracic surgeon and my mother is on the hospital board of directors. I'm currently building a family center wing at their hospital for children undergoing cancer treatments. It'll be a place where parents can stay with their children outside of the standard hospital setting, but still get the same topnotch care they deserve without all the beeping and white walls. State-of-the-art equipment, the latest technology, all of it."

His father raised an eyebrow. "Impressive. Sounds expensive. So, how did you two meet, considering it seems like you run in two very different circles?"

"It's nothing too out of the ordinary. We had a laugh over it at lunch with Tess and Nana, actually." Maggie chuckled, then took a sip of her drink only to come up empty.

Seeing his chance, Finn grabbed both of their empty glasses and rose from his seat. "We can save that story for the next family dinner. I'm getting Maggie a drink. Do you want one, Dad?"

His father's dismissive hand wave was all the reply he needed. Finn left the table and retreated through the kitchen door. Tess followed closely behind, her arms loaded with empty dishes. He'd left Maggie alone with the wolves.

Chapter Eight

Maggie was alone in a room filled with strangers. Her one safety net had left her. She'd kept a level head so far, but the sooner she could leave, the better. If anyone were to ask specifics, she might falter under the pressure. Deciding to turn Alastair's question around, she asked him, "What about you? What is it that you do now that you've retired?"

"I help Tess with Colin and the farm. After the accident, it's been hard to keep up with all the medical bills. Finn helps, of course, he's a good lad, but Tess wants to do it on her own, you know? She isn't the kind of girl who asks for handouts from her family." Alastair ruffled the boy's hair, who was deeply engrossed in expertly placing his peas in lines along the edge of his placemat.

Accident. Something else Finn had neglected to tell her about. Muffled shouts echoed from the kitchen. "I saw the workshop," she said, changing the subject and hoping to drown out the heated conversation taking place in the kitchen. "His boats are beautifully made."

"He has a special talent for it. I knew it right away as soon as he was old enough to help me in the shop. Put him right to work."

"I saw the picture of you two by his first boat on my way in."

Alastair laughed, grinning. "That was a great day."

"So I heard." Like father, like son. "Have you always been in the boat business? It seems to be a special niche here."

"Oh. We're on a few generations now, and I hope Finn's son will pass it on as well. People from all over New England are on his wait list for a specialty boat. Do you sail?"

"Mmm, a bit. At least, I did when I was younger. I don't have much time for it anymore. My father owned a gorgeous yacht, and he spent most of the year on it." In the always-sunny weather of California. "Well, the warm parts anyway," she added, hoping that would be enough to cover her tracks. "I was just telling Finn the other day how I'd like to show some designs to my father. I really think he'd be interested in buying." A good lie, but one that held truth. Her father would love something custom, she'd wager. And so would most of that social circle Alastair had mentioned.

She sat back in her chair, which groaned in protest from its weathered joints. Genuine smiles, hearty laughter, and love swelled to every corner of the room. These people, this *family*, truly enjoyed being in the company of one another. And they gathered on purpose. A twinge of jealousy bit at her as she watched those around her interacting at the table. The closest Maggie had ever come to having a family meal with her own was the weekend they'd been snowed in at the Hamptons during a freak late spring storm. The entire family had practically killed one another before the roads had been cleared. But this...*this*. She would take it in a heartbeat, if it meant getting to spend just one more day with her grandparents. She missed them terribly. Finn didn't know how lucky he had it. Annoyed as he was with his sister, at least she was here.

When the shouts from the kitchen grew too loud to ignore, Maggie pushed her chair back from the table. "If you'll excuse me." She placed her napkin beside her plate, pushed the chair back in, and inhaled deeply.

"You have any brothers or sisters, Maggie?"

She shrugged her shoulders. "Only child."

"Be careful getting between those two. You don't want to get caught in the crosshairs. I can't guarantee you'll make it out alive." Alastair flashed her a wink.

Warning received. "I'm a ginger. I got this." Maggie returned his wink and smiled, then made her way to the kitchen. It was set back from the dining room by a short entryway. The door was closed so she paused to listen before entering.

Dishes clattered. The pissed-off version of plate stacking. And then Tess said, "I'm sorry. I should have just kept my mouth shut." She didn't seem mad. She sounded...stressed.

"Yeah, you should have," Finn told her. "It's none of your business."

"When it comes to this family, it *is* my business." A rush of water drowned out the next bit of her sentence, but Maggie caught the end. "Because she's not going to find that here."

"What the hell? I know you're stressed about Josh, but you don't need to take it out on Maggie. She's done nothing wrong."

"Are you *sure* you didn't knock her up? I mean, how long have you known this girl? This is all so sudden. Something this crazy isn't like you. And you don't even *act* like a couple. I haven't seen an ounce of affection from either of you. If I were to pick two strangers out of a crowd and put them together, that would be you yesterday. And she didn't even know about Mom." Tess audibly choked down her emotions.

"It hadn't come up." Finn spoke softly.

"I'd like you to meet my parents. That seems like a pretty good time to bring it up."

Go, Tess. Match point on that one. Wife, fiancée, whatever she was... She should have been told, to save her from the humiliation. Too late for that. Maggie fought the urge to open the door, but maybe she could spare the two some hurt feelings. They shouldn't be arguing. Not over her.

"Despite the whole new name thing—I can overlook that just based on the fact you're a guy. But that rock on her finger? If you can even call it that. If you were to take a Starburst candy and turn it into bling, *that's* what it would be. No, a ring pop. A freakin' cherry ring pop." More dishes clinked and clanked. "I know business is good, but how much did that set you back? It's not even your style. You never flaunt like that. Ever."

"That woman out there—that incredible, phenomenal human being out there—I'd marry her again and again for the rest of my life, given the chance. I've loved that woman since the first time I met her and purposely spilled my drink all over her white sundress so that I'd have an excuse to talk to her. I remember the exact moment she walked into my life. It was eleven forty-three at night. I remember the way she constantly tucked this stray curl behind her ear, and how the tiny necklace hugging her collarbone shone like the stars in winter. So don't stand here and tell me what I should or shouldn't be doing with my life. I'd go to hell and back to keep her."

Maggie didn't know at what point she stopped breathing, but when her lungs screamed for a breath, she inhaled deeply, bracing herself against the wall with a trembling hand. No one had ever spoken of her like that. She'd never heard words spoken that sounded so true, so pure. Every fiber wanted to believe what he said was truth, but that shadow of doubt taunted he was just playing the part. Was he?

"You love her. I understand. But that ring is over the top."

"And it has absolutely nothing to do with you, does it?"

"I'm just stressed. And worried. Colin is going to need therapy for who knows how long, the horses are running out of feed, and the truck is on its last leg. Enrollment has been low this season. I was caught off guard and I'm hormonal. I'm sorry. I shouldn't have treated you like that or said those things. And thanks for the help with Josh today. I don't know what I would have done if you hadn't come. He was so drunk..."

"Tess, how many times do I have to tell you to just let me know when you need stuff? I mean, I know you wanted to do this on your own, but we're family and we are all in it together. Just let me help."

"Don't even start. You know how I feel about taking money from you. I'll contact that therapy school again to see if they want to partner. That should help."

Maggie's hand found her mouth and she pressed it softly against her lips. There was so much about Finn she didn't know. Voices lowered, and Maggie moved in closer, needing to hear his words. Then the kitchen door swung open, hitting her in the face. She let out a squeal and took a step back.

"Jesus." Finn exhaled sharply and his eyes widened.

"No, it's just me...Maggie." She laughed, rubbing the sting from the tip of her nose. "I was just...uh...drinks?" She bit the corner of her lip.

He took her palm in his, then tugged her away from the kitchen door, rounded the corner to the dining room and marched right through it, past two rows of gawking faces. They rounded yet another corner into a secluded, darkened room. He shoved the door shut behind them.

The sun had set during dinner, and the remnants of the day seeped through the windows opposite them. They were in a sunroom of sorts. Perhaps a converted sitting room, with two rocking chairs facing the windows and only a small table between them. A bowl of balled yarn sat on top of the table, and a book was cracked open upside down beside it. Faded floral wallpaper wrapped around the uneven edges of the walls. Doors on each side enclosed the tiny room, and they were alone. Just him, her, and the crickets warming up the orchestra in the grasses outside. The din of the dining room was but a distant memory. Just a low humming on the other side of the wall filled the void.

Finn's hands were stuffed loosely in his pockets while he paced near the windows. "How much of that did you hear?" he asked. He stopped midstep and turned on his heels to face her. "I'm sorry. Tess is…" His words trailed off with her approach.

"I understand," Maggie told him. And she did. Life wasn't always sunshine and rainbow-pooping unicorns. "It's not her fault. She's got a lot going on, and me showing up isn't helping her situation." She shouldn't be here. This family had enough stress as it was. "I really should go, Finn. I don't belong here. Not with you." The words seemed forced. "Your dad is right. We are two completely different people."

"Maggie…" he whispered.

"It's okay," she told him.

"Please tell me. How much?"

"Well, the ring pop part was kind of the low point for me."

He groaned. "So pretty much all of it, then. Look, it's just family stuff. Tess will understand once all of this is over. Colin was in a car accident about a year ago and the medical bills have been piling up, and I'm doing the best I can to help her out, and I don't know why I'm even telling you any of this, because it really doesn't even matter. She won't take my money no matter how hard I fight her on it. I'm at the point now where I'm just going to pay them and let her find out later. She's always been the stubborn one."

"She's right, you know."

"About what?" He turned toward her, just a shadow against the withering light.

"About us. Being different. It's kind of the perfect out for you. Think about it. You would realize what Tess was saying was right. It would never work, and we agree to go our separate ways." Without knowing it, Tess had given them the perfect opportunity to end this thing on a high note. "You should take the out she's given you." She sucked in a breath, then asked, "Did you mean it?"

"Mean what?"

"What you said in there. To Tess." She paused. "About me?"

He ran his hand through his hair, then turned his eyes upward. Without hesitation, he whispered, "Yes."

"Oh." The word escaped her lips on a sharp breath.

Finn turned, and in one step he was so close she could feel his warmth surround her. She took a hesitant step back only to be countered by his pursuit forward. With his every gaining step, she took one back, until she ran out of room. He leaned against the wall, trapping her between his arms. His forearms shook slightly, as if he struggled keeping himself upright. Or more appropriately, keeping them both from ending up in a compromising position horizontal in nature.

Maggie froze. Whiskey lingered on his breath, and she had no idea what his intentions were. A line had been crossed, and she wasn't exactly sure when or how, but she was certain it had been stepped over.

Bits of light reflected in his widened eyes like little flames licking at air. He moved in closer, if that was even possible. "What if I don't want an out?" he said, his mouth forming the words against the skin in the dip behind her earlobe.

"That's just the whiskey talking." The slight prickle-tickle from his unshaven face had her teetering on the brink of some sort of endorphin high. One teensy tiny push and she would plummet over the edge. Maggie needed to ground herself, but God, she couldn't remember the last time she had felt such a rush.

Vegas, that's where.

And with Finn. Did he have some super-human pheromone whose sole purpose was to crack her defensive wall and drive her mad? Cloud her judgment so much she'd fall right back into what got them into this predicament to begin with?

She pushed him backward and stepped away from the wall. She swallowed hard.

This was wrong. As much as it felt right, allowing it to continue was wrong. With a surge of determination, she distanced herself from him.

"God damn you, Finn." Her legs were jelly. She stumbled forward, tumbling back into his arms like she did it on purpose.

He swooped her up, hugging her close, and softly laughed. "Can't keep your hands off me, huh, Mags?"

The creaking of a door opening shot through her, and a flash of light filled the room. Maggie clamped her eyes shut and buried her face in Finn's chest to block out the abrupt change in illumination.

"Come on," groaned Tess. "This isn't the champagne room." She cleared her throat, then quickly added, "Finn, your friends are here." She left, leaving the door wide open and the light blaring down at them.

Maggie stifled a laugh. "She probably thought we were in here making out like teenagers behind the bleachers." Just peachy.

"Do you wanna?"

Maggie wasn't going to lie, she contemplated it. To taste

that whiskey on his lips just might sate that niggling craving she had for him. "I'm not going to answer that."

"Let her think what she wants to think."

"Your friends." He should go. She needed him to go.

"They can wait. Are we good?"

She nodded. "Seriously, we're fine. Go take care of your guests. I'll find my way there."

"Was that our first fight?" His charming smile hinted his tease.

Maggie rolled her eyes. *"Go."*

After Finn left the room, she managed to pull herself together enough to head back into the dining room. It was empty when she returned, and she was thankful she didn't have to face the entire entourage of friends and family. The table was partially cleared, so she stacked a few dishes and headed into the kitchen with them.

Tess stood at the sink with her back turned, laughing with her friend Jo.

"Maggie!" Jo cheered. "Come in, come in!"

She placed the dishes on the counter and smiled. "Just thought I'd help."

"Thank you." Tess smiled at her. "Really. It's hard to find good help these days."

"What can I do?" asked Maggie.

"You're too sweet," Jo said, wiping the clean dish Tess handed her.

"We got this," Tess told Maggie. "The game just started, if you want to play. They're all down at the paddock."

"Oh, I'm the least sporty person I know. I trip over air. I don't think anyone would ever want me on their team." Such truth.

"We *so* got this," added Jo. "First-time guests never have dish duty. If you want to go watch your guy, I get it, because he's way hotter than dishwater. But next time, you're on pots and pans, girly."

"Eww, that's my brother." Tess's nose wrinkled.

"Well, he is." Jo shot Maggie a wide grin.

"We'll be out in a few, so save us a seat, will you?" Tess plunged a pot into the sink, and soap bubbles erupted on her face. She blew air from the side of her mouth and brushed a strand of hair from her forehead with the inner part of her arm. "Dishes suck."

"I will." Taking her cue, Maggie left.

That hadn't been so bad. Actually, it had been quite friendly. She wandered through the house, hesitant to meander outside into the unknown. She moved from room to room looking at pictures, old books, and the mixing of a child's things strewn randomly around the house. She grabbed Finn's hoodie from the chair and slid it on, then found the front door. After giving herself a preparatory suck-it-up-buttercup talk, Maggie walked outside to be a cheery spectator for an overly glorified game of fetch.

Chapter Nine

The paddock wasn't hard to find. Tall lights illuminated the grand field in the distance. Not far from the house, a dirt path cut through the grass in the general direction of a barn, the field, and several fenced areas. A sharp chill bit at Maggie's shoulders, and she shuddered slightly, tugging the sweatshirt sleeves down over her hands. Maine weather was a far cry from California weather, where a jacket was more of a fashion accessory than a necessity. She followed the path to the field, passing signs stating safety rules, open ride hours, and various other things having to do with the horses and farm.

A large metal gate cracked slightly open provided entry to the paddock. She slipped through and took up residence in one of the higher bleachers, where there was room for a few tushies. Friends and family smiled, waved, cheered, and seemed genuinely happy to have her sit among them.

The makeshift baseball diamond wasn't full scale MLB-worthy, but the players seemed to be enjoying themselves. Laughter and a lot of taunting were being tossed back and forth between the two teams. Her eyes landed on Finn guarding second base, and he threw her a seductive smile. She turned her eyes away in a desperate attempt to not smile back like a teenybopper. She caught sight of Tess's son, Colin, next to the makeshift dugout in a child-sized wheelchair. A detail she'd missed earlier. Kai, from the grocery store, was doing some sort of hula dance in the outfield, and Maggie laughed. Such happiness surrounded her.

Tess burst through the gate and ran onto the field, taking a spot in the outfield. Her friend Jo wasn't far behind, but instead of joining the team, she made her way to the bleachers. A knitted shawl covered her shoulders and draped down to her waist. She looked like an angel floating up to the top row with her blond hair blowing gently around her cherubic face. She plopped down next to Maggie.

"Hey," she said, producing two mugs from beneath the shawl. "You look like you could use this."

The bold aroma of pressed coffee invaded the space between them, and Maggie inhaled deeply. "Oh my God, that smells amazing." She brought it to her nose. Heaven in a cup, delivered by an angel. She took a cautious sip from the steaming liquid, then followed it with a long swallow. "Oh, where have you been all my life? This is some seriously amazing coffee. I think I love you. I've been having some serious withdrawals."

Jo laughed then took a sip from her own mug. "Thank you, that means a lot. I make it myself. Even roast the beans. I own a little coffee shop in town. Cuppa Jo Coffee House. You should stop by sometime."

"Yes, definitely. A girl after my own heart. It's hard to find good coffee when you don't know the area. There's this hole-in-the-wall place I like to swing by when I'm on my way to work that makes the best espresso. Kind of out of the way, but so worth it. Winston always tells me to stay out of that area, but—" Maggie clamped her mouth shut. *Shit.*

"Coworker jealous you found it first, right? I like to keep secrets, too." Jo turned toward the game and Maggie felt inclined to do so as well, wondering just what secrets she was alluding to.

Content to watch the game, Maggie cheered with everyone else when a good play happened and laughed when Finn and his friends acted like stupid morons on purpose. Anything to impress the ladies. After unnecessarily sliding onto home plate, the guy Jo had brought to dinner kissed his fingers, tapped them against his chest, then pointed them at her.

"For you, baby girl!" he shouted.

Jo closed her eyes and sighed.

"He's a keeper, huh?" Maggie said when Jo pretended to gag.

"I don't know what it is with the men around here. They're great on day one but it's like they have this stupid switch that suddenly flips, and then they turn into a completely different person. Or I've pissed off the karma gods and am due for a terrible love life." Jo waved to her date half-heartedly before tucking her hand back beneath her shawl. "I need to get rid of him."

Maggie drank her coffee, wishing she knew how to commiserate with Jo. Finn seemed to flip that switch as fast as he could. Off, on. On, off. Even now, he couldn't take his eyes off her. Even from the expanse of field between them, she could feel his presence radiate around her. A warming glow that made her feel good.

Wanted.

And it was weird. Never in her lifetime would she have thought she'd be sitting in the middle of a pristine field watching a baseball game with a guy she'd had a careless fling with.

This game, surrounded by strangers, accepted as one of their own with *minimal* questions asked, she understood. Friday Family Fun Night. The evening wasn't about networking—no asking for a guest list before deciding on whether or not they'd be in attendance—it was about family and friendship. Just being in the presence of one another. She kind of liked it. The downtime was nice. She couldn't remember the last time she'd stopped to just take a breath and be in the moment.

"He's one of the good ones, you know."

Brought back by Jo's voice, Maggie straightened. "I'm sorry. I was spacing out."

"Yeah, you've been grinning like a fool for the last five minutes." Jo nodded in the direction of the field. "Don't let him get away like I did."

Maggie's coffee seemed to coagulate in her throat mid-swallow, and she coughed. Maybe even spasmed a little. "Oh? You and Finn?" was all she managed to choke out.

"We were high school sweethearts. He wanted me to stay, but I needed more. I wanted the whole college experience, you know? With the guys and the booze and the big city. So I left him here working in that shop of his and hightailed it out as soon as I could. He turned into a fine man, while I eventually came crawling back to my parents' house with a useless degree and no future. It's okay, though," she continued. "Because I have the coffeehouse and I absolutely love where I am in life right now. I could do without the losers, but hey. I'll pick my battles. I may not have found my Finn yet, but I can have fun looking. Girls have needs, too." Jo showed her a sly smile and wiggled her eyebrows.

"He's really great," Maggie blurted. *Is that the best you could come up with?*

"You are just what that man needs. I see the way he looks at you. He never looked at me that way. He'd part the Red

Sea if you asked him to."

God, if only Jo knew the truth. Jo seemed much more his type than she did, and her chest tightened slightly at the thought of them together.

Well, this was new. Was she...jealous?

Maggie was fraying at the seams. An overwhelming urge to have Finn near grasped at her, but she pushed it down. This was ridiculous. She was here for a divorce, not another weekend fling. Although, based on the way her heart raced when he smiled and the way her lady bits tingled when he pulled up his T-shirt to wipe his brow, exposing every ridge of that washboard, she found her plan questionable.

"I've always believed people are created in pairs, and we're destined to search the ends of the Earth to find our other half. You're lucky to have found each other again." Jo smiled and pressed her palm over her heart. "Romantic, right?"

There were so many ways Maggie could interpret that *again*. Everything from *She knows!* to just being analytical and overreacting. Paranoid. A dirty, dirty liar.

"Hey, Maggie!" Shouts and frantic waves from the field singled her out from the little group of spectators. "Hey! Come on!"

She pointed to her chest, as if there were another Maggie nearby, then shook her head. She was so not going to play baseball. She thought she'd made that very clear. In a last-ditch effort to ignore Finn and his friends on the field, she waved him off and asked Jo what she meant.

Jo pulled her shawl tight around her shoulders and laughed. "I take it you haven't seen *the boat*?"

Boat? What boat? "I... What?"

Finn wasn't having it. He jogged the distance between them straight to the bleachers and waved at her to come with him. "Come on. We need a batter. Bases loaded and we need an impartial player to bat for Colin. You're up."

"You do it. I'm talking to Jo." She turned toward her. "What... What boat?"

He bounced impatiently on his toes. "Maggie. Maggie. Mags. Come on. Maggie. Everybody's waiting. Don't disappoint a little kid. You'll ruin his whole life."

Damn, that man was persistent. If ever there was a conversation to be had, this one with Jo was it. What boat did she need to see, and why?

"Don't let me keep you. I'm just blabbering anyway," said Jo and shooed Maggie. "Go! Play! Have fun. They won't bite."

Finn shuffled impatiently while raising his arms over his head.

"I already told you baseball isn't my thing, Finn."

From the bottom bleachers, Nana, her sister, and a few others urged her to go. Their encouragement wasn't helping. It was doing the opposite—giving her the beginnings of an anxiety attack. The last thing she wanted to do was make a fool of herself in front of all these people. Maggie had never played a sport a day in her life. She didn't even know how to hold the bat.

Finn continued to press her. "I'm his runner. Come on. Colin wants you to bat for him. *Please...*"

"You're terrible, you know that?" Those puppy dog eyes could get him only so far.

Finn moved in closer, enough so he could rest his arms comfortably on a bleacher. And drill her with those eyes. "What...afraid to get those Louboutins dirty?" His mouth turned up playfully.

Maggie's jaw dropped, and Jo laughed.

"Yeah. I know things," he proclaimed with a little nod. "Do I have to da— "

"Hell no," she said, cutting him off. "Don't you even say

it." There was no way Finn was going to dare her to get out there on the field. Even if she looked like a clown, there was no way she could back down now. Not with everyone staring at her. Not with him pulling the kid card. "All right, smart-ass, let's do this."

Jo gave Maggie's shoulder a pat. "You can borrow my shoes if you want."

Maggie slipped off her heels and handed them to Jo, trading them for a pair of black flats. A bit snug, but they'd do.

"Ooh," Jo sighed, slipping into the heels. "I may never give these back."

Maggie hopped down off the bleachers and followed Finn to the field, doing her best to ignore the cheers and claps behind her. Finn led her over to home plate—nothing more than an old throw pillow—and handed her a metal bat. "Come on, slugger, show me what you got."

She could do this. She took the bat by the handle and gave it a little swing. "You know," she teased, "I could bust out a knee or two with one of these."

He raised his brows. "Louisville Slugger, huh? Know what you're doing?"

"Not a clue."

"Here," he said, coming up behind her. "Grip it like this." He showed her where to place her hands on the handle.

Maggie placed her hands over his. "Like this? I want to get this right."

"Perfect." He released the bat, then tugged at her hips lightly. "Now stick your ass out."

She straightened and turned toward him. "What does my ass have to do with hitting a ball?"

"Everything." He turned her back around away from him and pushed her forward slightly, back to her batting position. "Just trust me on this one," he told her. "You need the proper bat-to-butt ratio. Too straight and you'll never hit the ball. Too much and you'll fall on your face once you swing. It's really important you get the proper curvature to hit that home run."

She leaned forward, jutting her rear out slightly. "Oh my God, this is embarrassing."

"Not for me," he muttered, positioning her hips against his. His palm cupped her butt cheek slightly just before giving it a light slap. "Too much," he corrected.

She straightened a little, but he pulled her against him, pressing his business against her. Heat surged from him and through her, and her skin prickled as if she'd stepped out into a frigid winter wind.

He showed her how to swing the bat until she felt comfortable, and it wasn't until he let go of her that she realized she was standing in a field full of strangers with all eyes on her, waiting. And watching. Staring at her ass. And if that little show didn't have the stands convinced they were a couple, nothing would. Hell, he even had her believing it for a minute.

Finn jogged over to Colin and sprung him from his wheelchair. He twirled Colin around until he was carrying the boy piggyback and then wrapped his arms tightly around Colin's legs to hold him in place. Colin clenched his uncle's neck in an overzealous hug, and Finn took his spot in the direction of first base, ready to run.

"You ready?" the pitcher called out to her, winding up for the first pitch.

Maggie took a glimpse at the field. The bases were loaded and the outfield ready for her hit, gloves open. "Yes." She tightened her grip on the bat. "Wait." She thrust her backside out farther. "How's my ass?" she called to Finn. His belly laugh made her question her word choice—her present existence, really. She closed her eyes and let the words sink in. Bat-to-butt ratio. She'd fallen for it hook, line, and sinker. There was nothing else to do but show up and hit one out of the park.

Whistles and howls erupted with laughter around her. "Shake it, Maggie!" someone shouted from the outfield.

"Put your back into it, Mags!" Finn kicked at the dirt, copying her arched batting position.

"This bat is not a pole!" She challenged him but wiggled her butt anyway, then focused on the pitcher. She took up her best stance—ass out—and waited for the pitch, then swung.

A miss. The catcher threw it back to the pitcher. Strike one.

She inhaled, then let out the breath slowly. The ball was coming straight at her. She swung, and a jolt rang through her. She'd hit it!

Maggie dropped the bat and squealed as Finn and Colin shot off for first base. The runner on third raced toward her, and she jumped back out of the way as he pummeled through the pillow representing home. The second-base runner wasn't far behind. The outfield had retrieved her ball, but held on to it while Finn ran the bases—a sweet gesture for Colin. The boy's arms shot up in celebration as Finn rounded third base. Those in the stands cheered while his teammates gave him high fives as Finn jogged into home.

"Thanks for the home run, Maggie!" Colin chirped from his perch on Finn's back.

"You are *so* welcome, kid."

Finn lowered Colin to his chair and grabbed a beer from the cooler by the bench. He popped the top, then took a deep chug while the teams changed positions on the field. "Great job handling the equipment." He walked toward her rubbing his palm along his nape. "Do you want to play some more? I could probably find more balls you can play with."

Maggie let out a laugh. "I bet you could. While the offer

is tempting, I think I've had my share of the spotlight for today. I'm going to go sit and watch the rest of the game."

"All right, suit yourself." He leaned in and kissed her cheek. "One more inning and the game is over, but the offer will still stand," he whispered in her ear. "Any time, baby."

"You are so drunk, Finnegan Garrity."

His eyes narrowed. "I am not." Then he nodded. "Okay, maybe just a little bit." He pinched his thumb and pointer fingers together to show her his measurement of drunkenness. "Seriously. You're making me this way. It's not the beer. It's all you, babe."

"I'm going to go sit."

Finn slapped her ass, told her "Good game," and then jogged to his position on the field.

Maggie walked back to the bleachers shaking her head, not quite sure what had just transpired. This whole talking thing—being in each other's company—it was all too…*easy.* None of it had been forced.

As awkward as she felt putting herself out there, not once did she feel like she hadn't belonged. Everyone had been so patient while Finn showed her, rather sexually, how to hold the bat. And as much as she didn't want to admit it, she enjoyed it. Finn was fun. Something that seemed lacking in her life as of late. Where had all the fun gone? Her days were now filled with meetings, deadlines, and invoices. While the respite from reality was nice, chasing down "the big one" fueled her. Maine lacked the potential California oozed from its very core. And even now, sitting among some of the nicest people she'd ever met, she wanted to go home.

"Great hit, Maggie!" Eloise told her as Maggie passed by to resume her spot up by Jo. "We'll be having babies in no time!"

Maggie forced a smile and made her way back to her seat, but she couldn't shake the uneasy tightness in her belly. While

Jo spouted on and on about how amazing her Louboutins were, Maggie tried to make sense of the muddled memories swirling through her thoughts.

Why did everything have to be so easy when it came to Finn? Easy to stare at, easy to talk to, easy to just...*be*. No need to walk on eggshells. No constant fear of someone watching her every move. No one judging her.

Easy to forget why she was there in the first place.

She traded shoes with Jo, thanked her for letting her wear them, and watched the rest of the game with her knees tucked up under her chin and her arms wrapped around her legs. When the players left the field, those in the stands joined them for the walk back to the house.

The players gathered on the front porch for a drink, replaying the highlights from the game while most of the ladies headed back into the house. Finn grabbed Maggie's arm before she made it through the door and pulled her into his embrace. He leaned against the corner pole of the porch with his arms wrapped around her, keeping her warm against the evening chill. She squirmed, and Finn tightened his grip. "Gotta claim my girl," he whispered in her ear. "The guys won't stop talking about you." He kissed the top of her head.

"I think Maggie's ass shake deserves an instant replay," Jo's guy of the evening teased, taking a swig from his beer bottle. "Right in my face."

"*Dude*," Finn warned.

"I'm standing *right here*." Jo slapped the beer from his mouth.

"What?" He shrugged. "You're still my girl!" He leaned in to kiss her, but Jo planted her palm against his cheek, pushing him away.

"I am *so* not your girl." Jo brushed by him and through the door, leaving Maggie the only woman left with the group of drunken, horny men.

An uncomfortable vibe hit her square in the gut. "Can we go?" she asked Finn, breaking away from his hold.

"Yeah, of course," he told her, rising from his relaxed slouch against the porch. He led her through the house, saying their long Irish goodbyes as they found people. They were both hugged too many times for Maggie to be completely comfortable with, which was almost as bad as the wedding comments.

"Shotgun it."

"Wait a few years."

"Elope in Vegas and save the money for the honeymoon." Maggie had to laugh at that one.

She laced her fingers with his when saying goodbye to Eloise, because that's what a good fiancée would do, and when he said goodbye to his friends on the porch, his hold held fast.

"Boys, it's been fun. But when the missus says it's time to go, it's time to go." He lightly brushed his thumb over the length of hers a few times before letting go to do that bro hug guys did when saying goodbye. Cute.

Chapter Ten

Like a gentleman, Finn let Maggie take his arm for the dark and rocky walk to the Jeep. The night air hit her like a wall because she shivered slightly against it. "Is Maine always this cold?"

"It's that ocean air. Cuts right through you. Just wait until it snows."

She lightly laughed, saying, "I hope to God I'm not still here when it's snowing. I've never lived in a place with actual seasons. California has two seasons. Beach season, and heated pool season."

"What, no winter house in Aspen?"

"No, my mother doesn't like the cold." It took her a moment to catch on to his teasing. She lightly punched his bicep. "Jerk."

"Oh, come on, you walked right into that one." Finn fished his keys from his pocket and tossed them at her.

She was surprised she actually caught them but not at all surprised the driving fell on her, as she hadn't had a drink all evening. "Are you sure you want me driving this thing?"

"I asked if you minded so I could have a few drinks with the guys. You said it was okay on the way over here."

"I couldn't hear a word you were saying on the drive over here." So that's what he was babbling on about while she was smiling and nodding like a bobblehead figurine. "Oh, I don't feel comfortable driving this without you sober."

He faked a terrible British accent and gave her a grand sweeping bow. "Shall I have Charles bring round the Aston Martin?"

"Shut up." She took a deep breath. "Screw it."

She climbed up into the seat. California Maggie had been replaced with Maine Maggie, and Maine Maggie drove huge-ass Jeeps. She took off her heels, tossed them in the back seat, then buckled the seat belt, a bit unnerved the thin strap was the only thing keeping her from flying out of the missing doors. She slid the key into the ignition and turned it.

Nothing.

She tried again as Finn buckled in beside her. Still nothing. The engine didn't even turn over. "Uh, Finn? It won't start." Great. She'd broken it.

He stared at her for a moment before asking, "Did you push the clutch?"

"The what? Oh crap." The Jeep was a manual. She'd never driven one before, but she had seen it done in movies plenty of times. "You're going to have to tell me what to do, because the only thing I know about driving a stick shift is from what I've seen in the Fast and the Furious movies. And I'm pretty sure this thing doesn't have a nitrous switch."

He chuckled loudly, ending in a snort. "Punch the clutch, push the brake, pop it in neutral, and fire this puppy up."

She followed his instructions, turned the key, and the engine roared. Maggie gripped the steering wheel. The growl of the engine under her was exhilarating, she wasn't going to lie. Having that much power in her control felt amazing.

It wasn't all that often she was able to drive herself—her personal driver made good money toting her butt around.

"All right, now we're in business," she said, shifting it into gear. She released the brake, pressed on the gas, and the engine screamed at her. She let up on the clutch, the tires spun in the dirt, and the Jeep sputtered to a stall. She banged her palms on the seat. "This would never happen to Vin Diesel."

Finn unbuckled, then reached across the seat to unclick Maggie's seat belt. "Move the seat back," he told her as he began climbing over the center console.

"Oh my God," she laughed. "What are you doing?" She slid the seat back and Finn climbed in behind her, wedging her hips firmly between his thighs. "This isn't illegal or anything…"

"Ehh." He shrugged. "We did worse in Vegas."

"We are *so* getting arrested." Maggie went through the steps again, started the Jeep, then waited for further instruction from Finn.

"The trick to a stick is to treat it like you would a woman. You gotta make her purr."

"This conversation is quickly moving out of my comfort zone."

"Let your foot off the clutch nice and slow as you're giving her the gas."

Maggie eased up on the pedal.

"Yeah, just like that. And when you feel her starting to push back, that's when you change it up and switch gears. You'll be able to hear her, too. Just before she starts to scream."

"That has got to be the most sexualized description of a vehicle I have ever heard. Congratulations. You're officially creepy." The Jeep bucked a little, but she got it into second gear down the drive. As she reached the intersection to the main road, she slowed.

Finn quickly stepped on the clutch before she stalled out again.

"I guess I'm not cut out to please a woman, because there's no purring coming from this vehicle. I think it's actually in pain."

Finn's breath was hot on her neck.

"Get your mind out of the gutter." She looked both ways, then turned out onto the road. "And if you would kindly remove your package from my right butt cheek, it would be greatly appreciated."

He let out a laugh and readjusted himself.

"Seriously. It's a huge distraction," she told him.

He burst into a belly laugh. "That's what she said," he replied in between breaths.

"You did *not* just *she said* me, Finnegan Garrity." She swatted at him, hitting nothing but air.

"But you make it so easy." Just like that, he'd broken another barrier between them, allowing her to fall into a natural place of comfort. She couldn't remember a time when she'd had such...fun.

There were no street lights, no busy traffic jams. Just the black of night littered with the distant glimmer of stars and the melodic thrum of wildlife as the background music. Having grown up in Los Angeles, trees and lush green grasses were a luxury. She remembered having new sod delivered to her childhood home and the gardeners planting fresh flowers and shrubs every spring. It was the only way to have a bit of nature when you lived in a desert climate. She never thought it out of the norm until now.

Driving down these back roads, lined by enormous pine trees instead of towering walls of glass, was a scene from a movie. No copious amounts of exhaust or complete strangers screaming at one another over a foot of parking space or an extra five minutes on a meter downtown. Just space and sky.

Room to breathe. Dirt, and lots of it. Its pungency billowed intermittently between the open cavities of the Jeep. She inhaled a deep breath, filling her lungs with the salty sea air.

"At the stop sign, turn right."

Finn broke her thoughts, and she struggled to remember what gear she was in. The road was at a steady incline, and a large red stop sign beaconed from atop the hill. If she slowed down now, there was no way she was going to make it up there. Was she in third? Fourth? Dammit, what was the speed limit? Before she had time to react, Maggie was cresting the top of the hill.

"That's a stop sign," he warned her.

She squealed and blew through it, jerking the steering wheel to the right while attempting to shift and step on the brake at the same time, and failing.

"Oh, they're optional? Shit." Finn cursed, grabbing the wheel and the gear shifter to keep all four tires on the ground. "The next time I ask you to drive, remind me of that time we almost died, okay?" He slowed the Jeep, then allowed her to take over again.

Headlights in the distance grew closer. "Is that a cop? I think that's a cop. Oh, we're going to jail. I know it." Her palms began to sweat. "I am so going to prison. A butch girl named Melinda will make me her bitch and I'll be forced to wear orange. Orange is not my color, Finn. Don't make me wear orange." The car zoomed past. Her heart pounded in her throat.

"We're fine. Just keep going. We're almost there." He played with a curl next to her neck, using it to tickle the skin just behind her ear.

"Thank God, because by the time we get there I'm going to need a Xanax. Especially if you keep doing that."

He dragged a finger along her nape, pushing her hair to one side. "What, this?"

She swallowed hard against the dry lump taking up permanent residence in her throat. "Yep. That would be it."

"What if I do this?" His lips lightly grazed her earlobe. "Does that turn you on?" He wriggled behind her, adjusting himself in the seat. And she felt every inch of it.

Maggie concentrated on the road instead of the bulging package against her backside. "You need to stop, Finn," she warned. They weren't going to make it back to the house if he continued. They'd end up dead in a ditch or pulled over on the side of the road going at it, and neither was the optimal choice. She was doing her best to keep a level head, but the man certainly knew how to melt her with his mouth. He was dangerous with a capital D. Maggie forced herself to think of anything other than Finn, because unfortunately for her, she knew exactly what that D could do.

"Aww, I'm sorry, Mags. I let the whiskey go to my head." He backed off the touchy-feely nonsense and stayed silent, speaking only when she needed directions or help with the driving.

At the familiar sight of his house, she barreled down the rocky drive, pulling up next to her rental. She quickly shifted gears, came to a hard stop, and cut the engine, not caring that it stalled before she turned the key. She crawled out of the seat over Finn and gasped in a breath as if she'd been held underwater. Wrapping her arms around her middle, she headed for the house. Rocks and bits of dirt bit at the tender arches of her feet.

"Hey!" Finn called out after her. "Your shoes!" She turned to see him stumble from the Jeep holding her shoes upright above his chest. He yelled, "I saved 'em!"

Maggie bit the inside of her cheek in a feeble attempt to not show him just how much she appreciated his act of heroism. Although the sweet gesture softened her sexually frustrated exterior, she needed to remember why she was here. Despite how good Finn made her feel, they were grown adults now. She had a life.

She turned back toward the house, carefully choosing her steps.

"Maggie, stop." Finn breathed, catching up to her and cradling her heels as if he carried a precious newborn baby. "Let me get the door." He passed her the shoes and ran up the stairs.

As soon as the door was open, she headed for her room. Hot tears dangled on her eyelids, threatening to spill down her cheeks.

Finn caught her by the hand, spinning her around to face him. "Please let me apologize. I went too far with the whole PDA thing, and I'm sorry."

"This whole fiancée thing isn't going to work out." The words were forced from her mouth.

"I'm sorry I upset you. I... I thought we were on the same page here. The porch and the hand-holding stuff... Did I misread that? That felt...*real*. What did I do wrong?"

God, those eyes. Those beautiful, deep, soul-gutting eyes were staring at her, waiting for her to speak. He didn't get it. She blinked away a tear. A sob caught in her throat, and her voice cracked when she spoke. "That, Finn. *That* is what's wrong." She waved her arms toward the Jeep outside.

"Illegal driving?"

She pursed her lips, trying like hell to keep a smile at bay. She wanted to tell him just what he did to her. How, after all this time, falling for him again could be so easy, if only she'd let herself.

What was happening to her? She wasn't like this. She wasn't this person anymore.

Conflicted. Confused.

Her head swirled.

Because of Finn.

Butterflies flitted in her belly when she was simply near him. He was the culprit for her lack of common sense and levelheaded thinking. Call it voodoo, or witchcraft, or lethal attraction... Whatever it was, it stopped now. They would be friends. Nothing more. The past was the past. She'd moved on. She had a career now. Prospects. A promising future in California. Plans.

That didn't include him.

Chapter Eleven

It had taken Finn hours to fall asleep. The way things had ended with Maggie didn't sit well. His plan to show her a life with him had taken two steps back. It'd been going so well, and then she had stormed off to her room without so much as a second glance, leaving him standing in the dark like a drunken idiot. She was still in there, the Maggie he fell for all those years ago. He'd resigned himself to never seeing her again and had closed that chapter of his life. He'd braved Los Angeles, and it had shot him down once already—he didn't know if his heart could take such a beating again.

He'd hated everything about that city. The sprawling expanse of expressways and deadness. Just thinking about it gave him palpitations. How she did that day in and day out, he couldn't comprehend. Living as such was his worst nightmare. A sky without stars? Unfathomable.

For some strange, unknown reason, fate had pushed her back to him, and he wasn't going to screw it up this time. The moment when Maggie walked into his shop, he knew. He had to give it one last shot.

He woke with new purpose, kicking Operation: Win Back the Bride into overdrive. *Really* show her what life together could be. If he had only the weekend, he was damn sure it was going to be the best one he could give her. After a quick shower and some clean clothes, he was out the door before the sun rose.

He pulled into the parking lot of the supermarket with no idea what he was there for, but he was very thankful for the early bird hours. He was in and out in record time, weaving through the slow-moving swarm of senior citizens. He hit the register, paid, swung by Jo's place for coffee, and was back home before Maggie had even gotten out of bed.

She was single. There was still time to get her back. He'd start Operation: Win Back the Bride with food, Maggie style. Show her he listened and that he cared that *she* cared about plants and animals and stuff. He wanted to know the *why* behind that. It was something she was passionate about, and he wanted to experience it with her. A talk over breakfast seemed perfect.

She was clearly very upset; he was an ass, and he needed to apologize more. With food. Her kind of food. Fake food. Food pretending to be something it wasn't, like cheese made out of vegetables normal people had never heard of. He had no idea how to cook food that wasn't of the carnivorous kind, so he'd bought a variety of things from the very small specialty food section in the corner of the store.

Once back home, he spread the items out on the kitchen counter, contemplating what to make her. A veggie omelet with a side of...*something* molded into the shape of bacon strips would have to do. He could rock an omelet, but that was pretty much the extent of his breakfast abilities. His cooking skills were on par with his sixth-grade home economics class, but he was going to master this. How hard could it be?

The egg substitute needed no beating as it was already

in a gooey, gelatinous state straight from the container. The chopped veggies were simmering in a pan with the fake veggie bacon. Surprisingly, it smelled amazing. A hint of maple from the veggie-con bacon made his mouth water. As soon as the veggies were soft, the yellow goop pretending to be eggs went in a pan. He added the filling and folded over the egg perfectly. After shutting off the stove, he grabbed a plate from the cupboard, then slid the omelet onto it. A culinary masterpiece.

"Hey."

The omelet nearly fell to the floor. Finn quickly recovered and whipped around to see Maggie plopping into a chair at the table. "Good morning," he told her, placing the plate in front of her. "I made you makeup breakfast." He grabbed a fork and her coffee and placed them beside the plate. "I'm sorry about last night. I had too much to drink and forgot my manners. I was a jackass and my behavior was unacceptable. I put you in a terrible position. Please forgive me." He recited the words he'd been practicing all morning. "Did I mention I'm sorry?" He smiled overly wide, brandishing the cheesiest grin he could in hopes she wouldn't still be mad at him. "I brought you coffee."

She managed a smile and an eye roll. Her makeup-free face, still-sleepy eyes, and pouty lips that matched her flushed cheeks made her look like a goddess illuminating his kitchen. "Forgiven. Thank you for the breakfast and especially for the coffee." She grabbed the cup and brought it to her mouth and gulped.

And when she licked a bit of foam off her Cupid's bow with a flick of the tip of her tongue his knees buckled. "The vegetables are organic, and the bacon, well... I don't know what that is. But it's not bacon." He sat across from her. "I was going to get real eggs, but then I thought maybe you didn't eat those, either, because they're technically an animal, so I grabbed this carton of something claiming to be a substitute for eggs. I didn't taste test it, but it smells good, right?"

Maggie used her fork to cut a small piece and brought it to her mouth. She paused. "Are you going to sit there and watch me eat this?"

"Yes." His lips twitched.

She cautiously sniffed the food on her fork. "I've never had so many lies on a plate before." Maggie popped the bite into her mouth. She held it there for a moment, then her eyes widened and she shook her head. Her nose wrinkled and she spat the bite onto the plate. "Nope. No. Uh-uh."

"What? It can't be that bad."

"That bacon stuff is awful."

"The worker said the veggie-con was a best seller. People love it. Give it to me." Finn pulled the plate closer and took the fork from Maggie. He cut off a large bite and shoved it in his mouth. Artificial bacon flavoring overpowered his mouth, and he gagged a little. "Ugh," he coughed. "Oh, hell, that's nasty." He rushed to the sink to wash his mouth out. "Ugh, it burns." So much for finding his way to her heart through her stomach. Death by veggie-con wasn't the best way to jumpstart Win Back the Bride. "It's awful. I can't believe you eat that stuff." He wiped his tongue on a nearby hand towel.

"I don't." She took a sip of her coffee and leaned back in the chair. "If I didn't know better, I would think you're trying to poison me." She pulled her hair up, securing it with a tie she kept around her wrist. "Do you like pancakes?"

"Sure do."

"Me too," she said, standing. Maggie swooped in, taking over the kitchen. She rummaged through the cupboards, pulling out ingredients and spices and measuring cups and things he didn't even know he owned, like whisks and nutmeg.

He watched in awe as she glided around the kitchen like she owned the place, commenting on her food as if she were hosting a cooking show on the Food Network. All fun and lighthearted, and it eased the guilt he had about making her such an epic fail of a breakfast. He especially loved the way her tank top hugged her braless breasts, and he asked her to reach for as many items out of the cupboard as he could before she caught on.

Soon, a stack of the fluffiest pancakes he'd ever seen was placed before him. Melted butter oozed down the sides of the stack, swirling together with the warm maple syrup pooling along the plate's surface. He couldn't shovel it into his mouth fast enough. The deliciousness teased his mouth with every bite and he found himself licking the plate clean, wishing there was more. Finn placed the plate down only to find Maggie side-eyeing him from across the table. "I have no regrets," he told her.

She stood, pushing in the chair after her. "You missed a piece," she said, wiping his bottom lip with the pad of her thumb. She took his empty plate, placed it on top of hers, and brought them over to the sink.

Finn licked his lip, still tingling from the shock of her touch. What was *that*? Women were hard to predict. He glanced at the clock on the stove and scowled. He had work to finish up at the shop. Work that would more than likely take him the entire day. But try as he might, he couldn't make himself leave the table. He didn't want to leave her. He could spend the rest of his life watching her cute backside sway in the short little boxers hugging her ass if life would let him.

"Come to work with me today," he blurted out before he had the time to talk himself out of it.

"I may be able to cook, but you do *not* want to see me with power tools." Maggie busied herself straightening the counters while the sink filled with water.

She was washing his dishes. He should be washing his dishes. She was a guest. Finn pushed back his chair and closed in on the sink before he missed another opportunity to get close to her. "This is my mess."

"Nonsense. I need to earn my keep, especially since you probably spent a small fortune on all that food pretending to be normal food but that wasn't even close to normal. Or food. Bordering on murderous." She elbowed his ribs in jest and grabbed the dish towel from the counter. She threw it at him and said, "You can wipe, since I don't know where any of this stuff goes."

"I don't either," he replied.

They made small talk over dishes, everything from his business to the restoration of the barn-turned-house. She seemed to want to know all about him—what he'd been up to since they'd met last, and if he'd ever been back. They cracked jokes about Vegas, and Finn was thankful Maggie thought it was hilarious she didn't remember their most crucial time together, the fifteen-minute shotgun wedding they both thought was the best idea ever at the time. Hilarious, sure, but he couldn't help but feel a twinge of sadness she couldn't fully remember the single most vivid memory of his life. At least she wasn't mad about it.

He sighed. He needed to get to work. The boats weren't going to build themselves, and he had an order list that stretched out the door. "So, you coming or not?"

"What?"

"To the shop. You coming? I'd love your feedback on a few things." In truth, he just wanted her near. Being with her made him happy, and it wasn't a feeling he wanted to end. A natural high. Besides, there was no telling what she could get herself into alone in his house all day long. That would be detrimental to the Mission. He couldn't let her start thinking about the schmuck in California and the impending doom of Tuesday's meeting at the lawyer's office. He needed to show her just how amazing choosing him would be. What life together could be like. Just how happy he could make her.

She paused, but then said softly, "All right. I'd love to see what you do. I'll go get ready."

Relief flooded over him. He got to spend another day in her presence. And then it hit him. The best idea of all ideas. He would get her in a boat. She couldn't run away in a boat. "Wear something warm. We'll be out on the water."

She raised an eyebrow. "Doing what?"

Surrounding themselves with water on all sides, without distraction or people. "Seeing if the boat floats. Oh, bring a change of clothes."

"Why?" Her brow narrowed.

"In case it doesn't." She giggled at that, but he was completely serious. The boat he had in mind was a new design he'd been working on, and limits had been pushed on its dimensions. It had been sitting on a trailer for a week already, but finding the time to get it on the water to test it hadn't been at the top of his to-do list, what, with his wife showing up and all. Today seemed as good a day as any to give it a whirl. Hopefully the client would like it enough to pay for it. God knew he could use the cash.

A bag was packed, a few bottles of water stored in a small cooler with some ice, and both were tossed into the back of the Jeep. Soon they were rumbling down the road on the way to the boatyard. Classic rock blared from the speakers and wind ripped through the cab.

"You all right?" he asked her, ending the question with a small laugh while Maggie made a valiant effort to keep her hair from giving her whiplash. He reached around behind his seat and found a baseball cap, then handed it to her. "Here, try this."

"Thank you! You have an entire wardrobe in here!" she shouted above the music. "You'd think I would know better by now." She twisted her hair into some sort of knot and expertly tucked it under the hat and looked absolutely gorgeous doing so. So much so, he needed to remind himself he should be looking at the road and not at the tiny sparkling jewel hanging from her earlobe distracting him like a shiny fish lure. "Oh, I know this song!" Her face lit up and she turned up the volume, blasting out the lyrics to an AC/DC tune he was quite partial to himself.

He drummed on the steering wheel to the beat while she used her fist as a mic, and they finished out the song in perfect time as he pulled up to the shop. "Come on, let me show you what I've been working on." Finn parked the Jeep, unbuckled, and headed to unlock the door with Maggie at his heels.

He flicked on the lights and the workshop lit up. "Current project for a guy down in Mass. It's a gaff-rigged sloop with a jib-headed topsail. I've never personally made one before—this is a new undertaking—but I think it's coming along wicked good. My design is solid."

"Those are certainly all words," Maggie replied with a laugh, venturing deeper into the shop. "You'll have to show me with pictures." She stopped to look at every little tool, eyes wide, taking it all in. She picked up a scrap and eyed it curiously. "What's this?"

Finn stuck his hands in his pockets and sauntered in closer. "*That*, my dear"—he paused—"is a piece of wood." God, she was beautiful. Nothing turned him on more than a gorgeous woman and a boat in the same room.

"Oh, right," she replied, her cheeks flushing slightly. She set it back down and picked up the sanding block next to it. "And this?"

"Block sander. Wanna try it?" Finn grabbed a nearby piece of sandpaper and changed out the old one on the block for the new.

"You trust me enough to touch your work?" She gingerly

took the tool from him.

His eyes narrowed. "Of course. Relax. It's sandpaper. It's not like I'm asking you to rip planks through the wood mill. Give it a try." He waved her closer to the unfinished hull of the boat, then took her hand in his. He placed it against the closest beam. "Like this, with the grain," he said, tightening his grip to show her how to run the sanding block along the wood.

"How do you know how to do all of this?" she asked, rocking against him with each thrust and pull of the sander down the long grain of the wooden planks.

Back and forth. Back and forth. Driving him to the brink of madness.

"My grandpa taught my dad, and he taught me. It's in my blood, I guess you could say." He repositioned Maggie's hands to a different area not so far out of reach, if only to maintain some self-control and get her ass to stop brushing against his crotch. "And lots of trial and error."

"So... Were you building boats when we met? In Vegas?" She stopped briefly, turning to look at him.

"Mm-hmm," he answered, focusing more on how *not* to bring attention to the growing erection her hips were mere inches from exposing. He took a step back and adjusted his belt while her back was turned. He needed to think of anything but Maggie for a moment.

Dead puppies. Old lady boobs.

Dammit...boobs. This was not going the way he'd planned.

"You're good at this." She took over the work, continuing to sand the wood within her reach with full-on gusto and determination.

"What, sanding?"

"Teaching. Have you ever thought about it? Maybe opening a trade school or something? I read this article once about this huge shortage of tradesmen—"

"You are an ambitious one, aren't you?" He stood with arms folded lazily across his chest, content to just watch her work. Even with something as simple as sanding wood, she put her everything into it. He had to admit, it was incredibly motivating. He'd probably work that fast, too, if he had her in his shop every day. She'd end up making him look bad if he didn't.

"No, I'm serious," she told him, glancing over her shoulder. "It would be a great business opportunity for you. Is this your only shop? Have you thought about branching out? Teaching your methods to others could open new doors for you." She passed him the sanding block, placed her hands on both hips, and looked straight up. "Can I get in it?"

"Who said anything about opening new doors? Garrity Boatworks has been doing just fine right here in Rockport. It's practically a historical landmark now."

"But think about how many more boats you could build with a few more locations," she said, walking to the rear of the boat to where his work ladder was located. "There's an untapped market out there just waiting to be reeled in." She paused halfway up the rungs, then cracked a smile. "See what I did there?"

"Do you ever just have some fun without thinking about work? Be careful, that hull is just sitting in those bunks. They get tipsy." Her head disappeared behind the build, and he couldn't help but shake his head and smile. Her tenacity was something else.

She popped up suddenly, like a wind-up toy, resting her arms across the bow. "I *am* having some fun. Come on up, Boat Boy, the view from here is fantastic."

"The view of my shop is fantastic?"

"I didn't say I was looking at the shop." She peered down at him, her long waves framing the delicate curve of her face.

So that's how it was going to be? "Are you staring at my junk? Because I can explain that."

She laughed, leaning over the rail. "Come on!" She waved at him, then ducked back out of sight. The boat rocked slightly in its nest.

"Maggie, you need to be careful up there."

"It's really cozy in here!" Her voice echoed off the walls.

"It... What? It's not supposed to be *cozy*. It's a masterpiece," he grumbled, taking long strides to reach the ladder. He hoisted himself up far enough to see inside the empty hull. She was standing in the middle of his creation, her arms loosely wrapped around her middle. She stared up at the curvature of the beams in awe.

"She's beautiful," Maggie breathed.

"She certainly is," he replied, uncertain if they were still talking about the boat. Finn continued up the ladder, stepping inside of the wooden frame, careful to place his feet along the center beam. Maggie twirled in a circle as she continued her inspection of his work. "Maggie, slow down you're going to—" He lurched forward as the boat rocked sharply, using his body as a counterweight to keep the boat seated in the bunk boards.

In one swift swoop, he pressed Maggie to his chest as he rolled and fell to his back, landing unceremoniously against the beams. He coughed out a breath. His arms settled around her waist and he paused with eyes closed for a moment, just content to feel her warmth radiate through his body. Her chest rose and fell against him just as fast as his own, and he swore he could hear her heart pounding. He cautiously opened one eye and then the other.

Heaven stared back at him.

Neither of them spoke; he wondered if his time to crack a joke, or hell, even make a move, had passed. She seemed expectant—just waiting for *something* to happen, and he lay there, unable to even think straight. Her light floral perfume invaded his mind. Strands of her hair tickled the tip of his nose, the scent of her shampoo lingering inside his nostrils. His head lifted slightly, and he wanted nothing more than to kiss those pouty lips.

Maggie pushed herself up slightly with her palms and brushed her hair back behind her ears.

The moment was gone.

"See? Cozy," she said softly, unwrapping herself from him.

Her heat drifted from his skin, leaving behind a chill. He cleared his throat. "Right. Cozy." He stood and offered his hand to Maggie. "Come on, let's go get the trailer and get out on the water before you turn *this* boat into sawdust."

Finn locked up the shop, then drove around back to the boat trailer and hooked it up to the hitch in record speed. The sooner he got her on the water, the longer he could have her all to himself, without all the distractions of the shop.

"So where are we taking this bad boy?" she asked as he got back in the Jeep.

"There's a nice boat dock over on the other side of the lake by my house. The water's calm, only the people who live over there use it, and there's some shade along the tree line."

"Perfect for sinking, where no one will hear our screams. Got it."

He rolled his eyes. "Shut up," he told her, lightly pushing her shoulder. "Look at the bright side. If you're screaming, you're not drowning."

"What a confidence booster."

The drive to the lake was filled with loud, off-key singing by Maggie and Finn laughing until his sides hurt. When he backed the Jeep down the boat ramp, she was the first one out and ready to go. She even helped him unload. If she thought boats weren't her thing, she was mistaken. Maggie seemed so comfortable with the water. Such a turn-on.

With the Jeep parked in the lot and their bags stowed in the bow, she climbed into the boat, sitting on the far bench. "Wow. This is amazing. You made this?"

"Yep. Right down to the oars." The wood was smooth and soft in his hands as he rowed them farther away from the dock and out into the calm waters of the lake. This was his true home—his favorite place to hash over his thoughts. Sharing it with her was something out of a dream.

Maggie relaxed, leaning back against the side of the boat. His borrowed cap was pulled down low to keep the sun out of her eyes, and it fit her perfectly. Women in baseball caps were hot. Finn turned the boat toward the farthest point of the lake where the mainland was cut off by a small island that should be covered in wildflowers this late in the spring. He rowed in steady rhythm while she took in the scenery, her mouth slightly agape and eyes wild, reflecting the expanse of blue sky in their depths.

"Finn, this is beautiful. You're so lucky you get to live here and experience this every day."

You could, too, was what he wanted to tell her. Instead, he checked his position, adjusted his course, and glided through the water closer to the inlet. A calm breeze rushed over them, bringing with it the smells of spring.

Maggie inhaled deeply. "Who knew nature could be so therapeutic and calming?" She brushed a bug from her face with her palm. Then swatted. Then squeaked, "Oh God, it's a bee." She pushed herself backward on the bench seat, distancing herself from the flying pest.

The boat rocked slightly, and he adjusted the oars. "Easy there, Captain Ahab. Keep still. They can't see you if you don't move."

"It's a *bee*, not a T. rex."

"Seriously. They go after things that are moving. Sit still."

He reached out for her but the boat suddenly pitched to the left, and he quickly moved opposite to counterweight the rocking.

"No, you don't understand. I'm terrified of bees." Maggie ripped the cap from her head and used it as a weapon against the bee. Panic glazed over her face when it came at her with a death wish.

The boat rocked left. Then it rocked to the right. And before Finn knew what was happening, he was pitching forward trying to keep Maggie upright. He'd missed by mere inches. She flipped over the side of the boat and into the darkness. Water sprayed up into the bow from her flailing splash.

"Maggie!" he called out. Leaning over the edge, he searched the murky depths of the lake for her. His stomach twisted. *Come on, Maggie.* He checked the other side of the boat, hoping he wouldn't find her floating face down from anaphylactic shock or drowning from hitting the cold water like a punch to the gut. His heart leaped in his chest.

Nothing.

Could Californians swim?

"Maggie!" He raised his voice, hoping she'd respond. Then she crested the surface of the water, her red hair cascading down her back like The Little freaking Mermaid, spitting water at him. She sucked in a gasp of air and wiped the drops from her eyes.

"Is it gone?" she asked him while treading water a few feet from the boat.

"Yeah," he told her, exhaling. "You scared the crap out of me."

"Sorry. I wanted to make sure it was gone." She swam to the edge of the boat, taking hold of the edge. "This water is stupid cold. Are there *things* in here?"

"Did you get stung?"

"No, I think I fell in before it had the chance to kill me. Those little kamikaze bastards have no business having needles attached to their butts." She attempted to keep her teeth from chattering and laughed. "You should come on in. It's like bathwater in here." She floated onto her back and stroked her arms back and forth like a synchronized swimmer. *Adorable.* And that light-colored, flowered, soaking wet, clinging-to-her-body-like-Saran-wrap shirt showed everything. *Ev-ery-thing.*

"Yeah, no thanks. Here, give me your hand and I'll pull you back in." He reached out for her, extending his arm far out over the edge so she could reach.

She grasped for him. "I can't get you. Oh God, something just touched me." She swirled around erratically.

He inched out farther, stretching his frame over the water. "You can do it. You're almost there." He wobbled slightly but caught himself before ending up in the water next to her. There was no point in both of them getting wet.

She took hold of his wrist loosely, allowing him to pull her closer to the boat. As he let go of the oars to grab her with both hands, she rose up out of the water and wrapped both of her sopping wet arms around his neck.

And pulled.

Finn hit the water face first. Water, so cold it gave him an instant brain freeze, flooded his ears and nostrils as he tried to right himself under water. He breached the surface, exhaling in short bursts. His balls shrank to the size of raisins, and his lungs couldn't fill to capacity, but Maggie was laughing at him, and her smile was genuine, so he suffered in silence. Hypothermia was worth it. "'Come on in,' she said. 'It's like bathwater,' she said."

"Payback's a bitch."

"For what?" he asked, treading water beside her.

"*Veggie-con.*" She splashed water at him.

He splashed back and laughed. "It sounded like a good idea at the time."

"Yeah, if you're looking to secretly murder someone."

Waves from a nearby boat rocked them in the water. The boater slowed as he neared them, cutting his motor. "Do you need some help? Is everything all right with your boat?"

"We're good!" Finn told the man.

"Oh, you know. Just seeing if it floats," added Maggie.

"You have an interesting method, for sure. And that's a beautiful craft you have there." The man tipped his straw hat and continued on.

Finn swam toward his boat, riding the wake of the man's waves. "Come on. I'm freezing my nuts off." He heaved himself up over the rail of the boat and flopped into it, thankful to be out of the bitter water, although the cool breeze ripping through his wet jeans didn't help with his nut size. After pulling Maggie in, he took up the oars and headed toward the island as fast as his arms would let him row.

When he reached the shore, Finn jumped out and pulled the boat in, then helped Maggie to disembark without having to get in the water again. He grabbed their bags, took her by the hand, and led her down a narrow walking trail through waist-high wildflowers and tufts of grasses.

When they reached his favorite clearing, he tossed the bags down and sank to the ground. On the slight incline of the hill, most of the lake was visible. The quiet calmed his soul. The buzzing in the trees was the only music he needed. He sighed, taking in a breath to fill his lungs. There were no roads, no cars or storefronts. Just him, nature, and the water. And Maggie.

She dug through the bag with the dry clothes, pulling out hers. "You know, this would be a perfect spot to have a little picnic, don't you think?" She tugged her top up over her head and slid out her arms, revealing a light pink, lacy bra without a second thought. "Chilled wine and cheese under the stars. Ooh, melted brie with a brown sugar and whiskey sauce drizzled over fruit. Is that a thing? I feel like that could be a thing."

She stood there in just a bra and wet pants, totally oblivious to the fact he was now crossing his legs to keep her from seeing his man goods doubling in size while she was talking about picnics. *Picnics.* He attempted to break his stare, but everything else seemed impossible.

Damn, she was beautiful. Porcelain skin and curvy in all the right places and just...perfect. Somehow, she managed to take her wet bra off and replace it with a clean one under her new shirt without taking it off or showing any of the good parts like it was some elusive magic trick. The same went for her pants. The wet ones were replaced with the tiniest thong that shouldn't even be labeled as underwear, as there wasn't enough fabric to leave anything to the imagination, and a pale pair of blue jeans he wanted to run his palm over just to feel their softness against his skin. And rip off with his teeth.

Maggie lowered herself to the ground beside him. "Are you going to change?"

"Nope." He shifted his weight in the grass, hoping the movement was subtle enough Maggie wouldn't realize why his jeans were so tight.

"That one looks like a pineapple," she said, pointing at the clouds.

"It looks like an old man ass, blowing out a fart."

She rolled her eyes at him. "That escalated quickly."

He just laughed. "Well, it does."

"You couldn't have said Sonic the Hedgehog or a cute little pony? Boys are so gross." She elbowed him in the ribs. "Can I ask you a personal question? It's probably rude of me to ask, but I feel like I should know."

"Shoot," he told her, really hoping it wasn't anything

having to do with past girlfriends, his sister, or his complete lack of culinary skills. Every spoken word between them made him nervous. Like middle school all over again. He didn't want to say the wrong thing or act like an idiot. None of that punching a girl because you like her crap.

"I know you said he was in an accident, but what happened to Colin? Why is he in a wheelchair?"

Or family. Especially stories that weren't his to tell. He let out a long breath. "Well, long story short, Colin's drunk sperm donor decided to pick him up at the house and take him for ice cream. Tess was running a therapy session down in the paddock, my dad was at the shop, and Colin was supposed to have been in the barn with the guy who worked there. Before we knew it, the police were at the house telling Tess there had been an accident. The asshole walked away with just a few bruises, but Colin wasn't buckled in the front seat and has spinal damage. He's getting there, but his recovery is slow."

He heard Maggie swallow hard against her staggered breathing. "That's terrible. I'm so sorry. I shouldn't have asked."

He shrugged. "It is what it is. If I could go back to that day and change it, I'd gladly take his place. Any of us would. But that can't happen, there's nothing we can do about the past, so we work on the future. I try to help as much as I can, but it's hard to understand. There haven't been very many options around here for the therapy he needs. Rockport is small, and it's hard for Tess to get him down to Portland to see the specialists. It's a two-hour drive one way, twice a week. So we take turns when we have to."

She was quiet for a while, staring at the clouds and fiddling with a piece of grass between her fingers. "I understand. I wish I knew a way to help Tess and Colin. With all the love in your family, you'll find a way. I know what it's like to want to help people but not know how. That's why I do what I do.

If I can change just one life, help just one person, I know I've made a difference. The project I'm working on right now... All proceeds and donations are going to free family housing for children undergoing treatment. Families shouldn't have to worry about paying for a hotel while saving their child's life."

His head turned toward her, finding her eyes. "I commend you for doing what you do. Not enough people care about those who can't speak up for themselves. You have a voice, the avenue, and the drive. It's really something special. Don't let people tell you any different."

Maggie smiled. "Thank you."

A part of him wanted to tell her about his trip to California. How he'd seen her in action and how awestruck he was just to have been in her presence. But security had escorted him out fairly quickly once her father had found out who he was. Her father had thought he didn't deserve her.

But that was then. Here and now, he knew she could do great things, and something inside him tugged at his heartstrings. She could do great things anywhere... But would he only be holding her back? He had his own thriving business, but he lived in the middle of nowhere. He didn't need an internet connection to run power tools, and even the most reliable company's service was spotty, at best. Hell, he didn't even own a TV.

His wellbeing was as unplugged as Maggie's was connected. The closest city was a two-hour drive away and small, at that. Certainly not what she was accustomed to. He was content on the ocean. He loved his job. He loved the life he'd made for himself. She loved the city. She loved the hustle and bustle of it all. Could he really take all that away from her? He second-guessed his plan. His conscience ate at him. But he had to know for sure.

She tossed the blade of grass above her and blew it away

with puckered lips that made the most perfect kissy face he'd ever seen.

"So, you come here often?" she asked, grabbing another blade of grass and repeating the entire process, puckered lips and all.

"That is the lamest pickup line I've ever heard. Is that the best you could come up with?"

"That *so* wasn't a pickup line." She folded her arms behind her head to make a pillow.

He wanted to bring her here often. Every day. Share private moments together, just like this one. "Did you ever build a blanket fort and hide from people when you were little?"

"Sure."

"Well... This is my blanket fort." He spread his arms open toward the sky.

She turned her head to the side, facing him. His eyes caught hers. A soft smile curled the corners of her mouth. "Thank you for sharing your blanket fort with me."

Chapter Twelve

Maggie stretched her arms over her head and arched her back, pointing her toes downward. She yawned and fluttered her eyes against the waning afternoon sun. Her sights settled on Finn, bare-chested, his tanned body glinting under the remnants of daylight.

"Welcome back, sleepyhead." Finn zipped up his jeans. "You missed the show. I did a little dance and everything."

"Aw, I missed the little dance?" She pushed up onto an elbow. "That's the best part." Her stare traveled farther south, to the loose fit of his jeans hugging that sexy vee of his hips.

"Hey, naked over here." He crossed his arms over his pecs.

Heat flushed her face. "Sorry, I, umm…" Didn't know what to say. There was no recovering from that blatant ogle she'd given him. But a masterpiece was hard to resist. God, she was weak. And he was hot. "The Carlton or the Hammer Dance?"

He cocked his head to the side in thought, then smiled. "Maybe a little bit of both."

So freaking hot.

"Might have even thrown a few hip thrusts in there, but I

guess we'll never know, will we?"

Maggie stood and brushed the stray leaves and grass from her clothes and ran her fingers quickly through her hair. She could only imagine what she looked like. Probably favored a drowned rat. "We should be getting back," she told him. "Don't you think? It's going to be dark soon, right? I don't think I could get used to how different it is here."

"The moon on the water is the best part."

"If I fall in again, I'd like to be able to see where I'm drowning."

"I won't let you fall," he said, his voice low and soft.

And she absolutely believed it. The sincerity in his eyes rattled her. Shook her insides to her very core. Everything she had been sure about in life now teetered on a crumbling ledge. He stretched his hand out to her, and she took it, slipping her palm into his. His fingers curled around hers and held fast. She let him lead her down the path back to his boat, and laughed when he swept her off her feet and plopped her inside it so she didn't have to get wet.

"So gallant." She righted herself on the bench seat.

"I try." He shrugged as he pushed the boat away from the shore and hopped in. "Don't worry, darlin'." He started to row. "I wouldn't toss you in. I wouldn't do something like that." His lips twitched as he tried to hold back a smile. "Probably wouldn't."

Maggie tucked an errant lock of hair behind her ear before leaning forward to rest her elbows on her knees and her chin in her cupped hands. She was smiling. How long had she been smiling at him? She sat up again, but couldn't make herself stop. She took her bottom lip between her teeth and bit down, but it did nothing to stop that tingly feeling bubbling up inside her.

What was this? What was going on with her? Was this what it was like to be carefree and happy? No phone, no agenda, no one breathing down her neck about deadlines and money. She'd enjoyed her day. Even the almost drowning. She didn't even have to play a part. Although a not-so-pleasant feeling swept over her when she realized she probably had fifty missed calls by now and a dozen voicemails filled with panic, asking why she wasn't returning calls or picking up the phone. She'd be surprised if they hadn't sent out a search party. Too bad no one knew where she really was. But she wouldn't put it past some of her partners to track down her location via GPS.

The trees buzzed with nature's nightlife, complementing the steady *swish* of the oars dragging through the water. Finn slowed when they approached the dock. An older man was tying up his own boat on the opposite side. The dock lighting illuminated his shadow, making him seem ten feet tall against the water.

"Hey, Abe," Finn greeted, pulling up alongside the dock.

"Well, hello there, neighbor!" The man tipped his hat with knobby fingers. He was in his upper years, but seemed to be still in good health and strong, seeing as he was tying up his own boat with ease. His white hair gleamed under the light.

Finn stepped out of the tippy craft and tied it off. "What are you doing out this late? Getting a little dark for fishing, isn't it?"

Abe chuckled. "Just getting away for a bit. Mary's having a little shindig up at the house. Sixty-fifth anniversary or whatnot. Cake, and all that. She was going to give me an aneurysm if I didn't get away while they were setting up."

"That long, huh? That's something to celebrate, Abe. Happy anniversary." Finn patted his neighbor on the shoulder.

"You and your lady friend should stop by. Mary would love to see you. Who is this beauty you're hiding all to yourself over there?"

She waved. "I'm Maggie."

"Well, Maggie, my dear, convince this boy to twirl you around the dance floor and make this old man happy. Please say you'll come."

The strangers in this town sure knew how to tug at her heartstrings. "We'd love to."

Abe slapped Finn on the back. "I'll tell Mary. I need to get back to the house before she sends out the hounds. I'll see you both there." Abe waved goodbye and set off down the road, away from the boat ramp.

"You have no idea what you've gotten us into." Finn smoothed the scruff on his chin and laughed. "Clear your schedule."

"Oh, come on. He's adorable." Maggie grabbed the bags and stepped up onto the wooden planks of the dock, testing her land legs. "It sounds like a good time. And there's cake. I love cake."

"*Cake* cake? Or...cake?" The sexual innuendo was strong.

Maggie hesitated, contemplating her answer. "Depends on the occasion."

He shook his head at her and sighed. "I'll go get the Jeep."

"Oh, come on, Finn. Live a little. Did you have other plans for tonight? Other than to sit in your house and watch the TV you don't own? I don't feel like going home just yet." She raised her hands up toward the darkening sky. "I want to see this place. Experience this small-town living. Meet the people!"

"Just... Let me get the Jeep before you go all *Sister Act* on me."

He had the boat loaded onto the trailer with the speed and expertise of a master of his craft. She watched in awe as he latched the straps tight. How the rolled cuffs of his shirt strained around his biceps. How she wanted to rip his shirt off to give those guns some breathing room. How his hair had dried in unkempt waves and how the muscles in his thighs filled out his jeans in the most exquisite way.

How he smiled at her. With his whole heart and soul.

God, it pulled at her.

"What?" he asked, rubbing his palm along his nape.

She shook her head. "Nothing. I'm not used to this disconnect. It's just… It's been a good day." She climbed up into the Jeep.

"Yeah," he told her, starting the engine. "It has. I was thinking about taking you to the ocean. Show you how to find the pearls inside of mussels. I used to smash them to pieces with rocks when I was a kid. Great stress reliever. Not so much for the mussel, though."

"That sounds…brutal. Do you know what I could use right now?" She stared at him intently.

"What?"

"Coffee. I need coffee."

Finn rubbed his eyes. "You need an intervention."

"Coffee and I are in a committed relationship, and that isn't even describing it properly. That first sip in the morning, it's a religious experience. 'You want coffee?' is my love language. It's that serious."

He snorted. "I'm sure there will be coffee at Abe's and you can get your fix."

The drive to Abe and Mary's was only a few minutes down the road along the edge of the lake, but the silence and awkward glances between them made those minutes almost unbearable.

Something had changed between them. She didn't know exactly when that had happened, but it was there, hanging in the air. Change that wasn't necessarily a bad thing—just different. Finn parked the Jeep out of the way so the trailer wouldn't be in the way of traffic, and they walked the length of the drive. They made small talk, and his lighthearted jokes about the day set her mind at ease until the muddled drums and the humming of lights and music rolled through the air.

She stopped. "Maybe I didn't think this free-bird version of me through." She curled her arm around his, her palm settling on the inside of his bicep. "I feel like we're intruding. These people don't know me. Abe was just being polite. This is one of those *I'm inviting you only because this is awkward* situations, isn't it?"

"Nah, you'll love them. And they'll love you. They're some of the best folks I know. You'll fit right in." He took her hand in his and led her down a stone pathway to the garden in the back of the house. A beautiful wooden trellis dripping with lavender wisteria and twinkling lights beckoned them closer. "They may be old, but they know how to throw down a party."

The secret garden gave Maggie pause, and she gasped from the sheer beauty of it all. It was something to see. Nostalgic and ethereal and classy all wrapped up in a neat little package. Maggie had seen some swanky events but nothing such as this. A tall weeping willow tree edged the far corner of the property, and its swooping branches were drenched in soft glowing bulbs that reminded her of the lightning bugs she used to chase as a child on their summer trips to the Cape. A rock wall lined the edges, trimmed with a vine hedge. A balcony jutted out from the wall overlooking the lake. A duet of crooners sang sweet melodies from atop a small stage backing up to the house, and a wooden dance floor covered the grass. Wrought iron tables with matching chairs hidden in the corners looked rather cozy under the willow tree.

This backyard, barely the size of just one of many rooms Maggie booked for events, put every job she'd ever taken to shame. The simple elegance reminiscent of times gone by was breathtaking. And it lit a fire in her chest.

"This…this…" She wanted to do this. Be a part of this. Capture this feeling and bottle it. "This is spectacular."

"This is how we do events here." Finn ushered her to a table filled with hors d'oeuvres and a towering four-tiers cake. "Hungry?" he asked, picking up a plate and passing it to her.

"Starving." Maggie took the plate, piling it high with desserts, fruit, and some sort of bite-size quiche that looked too cute to eat. Finn grabbed everything meat-related and two glasses of blush wine, then found them an empty table beneath the glimmering willow. "So good," she murmured, shoving something chocolate in her mouth. The older couple in the middle of the dance floor caught her attention. They gazed adoringly into each other's eyes and slowly swayed with the music. "Is that Abe and Mary?" Abe's flannel shirt and loose-fitting jeans had been replaced with a black suit and tie.

Finn nodded. "Sixty-five years of putting up with each other and loving every minute of it."

A sadness swept over her. To have a love like that. Evergreen.

Maggie would never have that. Not with Winston. Not in California. Not with the expectations she was supposed to uphold. She would do her duty as her family requested. Marry within the society circles and mark her place among the privileged. Doing so was her *in* to all the places. Fancy parties. Dinners. Places to schmooze. Having access to certain environments and the people within them ensured she had enough donors for her projects, specifically her hospital wing. Sometimes it was messy and unforgiving, but she was going to do what she had to to fulfill her dreams.

But it wouldn't be with Winston. The keep-your-enemies-closer deal. He wasn't the one for her—a stark reality she needed to come to terms with. Her girlish hopes and dreams were just that. They would never be Abe and Mary.

The couple kept up with the beat, and Abe even gave Mary a twirl before pulling her back into his chest to hold her close. "I'll be looking at the moon but I'll be seeing you," the crooners in the band sang.

"Abe convinced Mary to get hitched the day before he shipped out for the war. This song kind of became the theme song for all the women waiting for their men to come back home. Standing there on the railway platform, possibly seeing your lover for the very last time. Nothing but hope and a rare letter to keep you going. Never 'goodbye,' always 'I'll be seeing you.'"

"That's incredibly romantic." Maggie crossed her arms and leaned on the table, content to watch them dance and truly love each other in the moment, the here and now. Never guaranteed a tomorrow. She lost herself in the song, listening to every word. *I'll be seeing you.*

The song turned from endearing to a faster-paced number.

"Mmm!" Finn slapped his palm on the table, snapping Maggie to attention. He swallowed down whatever he had in his mouth, licked his finger, and stood. His chair scratched against the stone patio and wobbled dangerously on two legs before settling back to all fours. He reached out for her. "Dance with me."

"He dances? I get to see your little happy dance? Why, Finnegan Garrity, I do declare!" Her hand went to her chest in overly dramatic feigned surprise when Finn busted out his best dance moves—the swingy Carlton straight into a shuffling Hammer dance rendition that would rival any nineties cover band. She took his hand, her exuberant laugh surrounding them both.

He spun her in a fast whirl, wrapping her in his arms. She swayed along with him, her back pressed against his chest until he unwrapped her. His palm slid gently from the curve of her shoulder to the small of her back. With just a simple touch of a hand, he had her undivided attention. The devilish gleam in his eyes met her shocked look as he took the lead, sweeping her effortlessly around the dance floor. He was testing her, switching up his moves from a jazzy swing dance to a modified waltz, and Maggie effortlessly kept pace, matching him step for step. Two could play this delightful game. If he thought he was going to make her stumble or mess up, he had another thing coming. She would win this one. All those years of dance lessons her mother made her take would finally pay off.

"He dances," Finn confirmed, pulling her in to him. He exhaled deeply.

She won the silent dance-off. She laughed, wrapped her arms around Finn's neck, then pressed her cheek against his beating heart.

"I thought for sure you were going to give up," he said. "But I don't have much left in me."

"Your heart sounds like it's going to explode."

"I'm not entirely sure it isn't." He cradled her with a new tenderness, his fingers gently caressing her back in slow, rhythmic circles.

The song came to an end, and Abe joined the singers on the platform, taking over the mic. "Hello, everyone, and thank you for joining my lovely wife and me tonight. We are so happy you could join us to celebrate the best sixty-five years of my life." The guests clapped, and Maggie broke her embrace from Finn. "Now," Abe continued, "this is a little tradition Mary and I have, and we'd like to share it with you all here. Who here has been married the longest? Other than myself. Anyone?" Laughs and names were called out from the guests, all nominating who they thought the couple should be. They finally decided on Abe's brother and his wife. "Get out here on the dance floor, you two," Abe told them. "And who is the newest married couple here? Anyone under ten years? Five?" He searched the crowd.

"What about Finn and his fiancée?" Someone shouted

from somewhere along the sidelines. "They're newly engaged. That should count, right?"

And then Abe pointed straight at her. "Yes," he said with conviction. "Finn and his fiancée, Maggie, everybody!"

Maggie wasn't one for the spotlight. Especially not at something like this. They'd gone from invisible guests to the stars of the show in under sixty seconds.

Finn guided her across the dance floor and took her in his arms. Her hand found his, his fingers curling around hers in a reassuring embrace. And there they waited for the music to start while the crooners conversed with the band. The lights strung above the dance floor turned into tiny little balls of scorching heat. Sweat beaded along her nape.

"This is so awkward," she murmured.

"Eyes on me," Finn whispered low in her ear. "It's just you and me and this song. And a few new moves. Try to keep up." He straightened his form, morphing into a professional dancer, and all business.

They were off, floating around the floor in the most beautiful mash-up of ballroom dancing she'd ever been a part of. At every turn and twirl he upped his game, flitting from a foxtrot to a Lindy Hop and back again. She matched his every step.

"So that's how it's gonna be, huh?" She laughed, squealing when he tipped her backward in a low dip. From upside down, she saw legs. Lots of them. A crowd gathered along the edges of the dance floor. "Everyone is looking at us."

"Really," he chuckled, his eyes never leaving hers. "I hadn't noticed."

The singing paused for a transition, and the attendees clapped and hooted. Finn placed his hand along the curve of her nape. The twist in her hair had come loose at some point during their dance-off, and he now buried his fingers in it before slowly bringing her upright.

Short breaths escaped her lips, and she placed her head against his chest, his palm still cupping her neck. She closed her eyes. His heart beat erratically beneath her ear, drowning out the music with its own overwhelming bass. Aromatic blends of wildflowers, sweets, wood, and water melded together, lingering in the threads of his T-shirt, beckoning her to move in closer, if even possible.

Finn hummed along with the music, then melodically muttered, "How wonderful life is, now you're in my world," subtly changing the words from the eloquent ones Elton John had written. His lips found her ear. "Stay," he whispered, his breath warm against the evening ocean air.

She tensed in his embrace. Her very being told her to walk away. Run away.

She looked at him to speak, to tell him to stop, but when she opened her mouth, nothing but a squeak bubbled out from her mouth.

"I mean it," he told her. "It wasn't just a dare for me."

"I...I..." She hadn't expected this. Watching his lips move with the words entranced her. She wanted to taste them. Cover them with hers. Feel that thrilling rush invading her senses.

Finn cupped her chin. "Give me a chance. If I'm not the one for you, I'll sign your papers, no questions asked. You walked back into my life for a reason. There's something between us. You can't tell me you don't feel it."

This wasn't happening right now. It couldn't be. This was just a dream. They were dancing in a dream, and any moment now she'd wake up. His eyes searched hers. Honeyed and gorgeous and breaking her, piece by piece.

She pulled away from him. "This isn't some game. I'm not here to have fun. It's *this* that's putting ideas in your head," she told him firmly, waving her hands in the space surrounding her. "It's gotten to you. *This*," she said, pointing back and forth between them, "isn't going to happen. So put whatever ideas you have of me to rest. I'm sorry if I've given you the wrong impression, but I'm here for a divorce. Not a rekindling of some mistake. If you'll excuse me, I need a drink."

Somehow, she managed to break free of his spell and found herself heading toward the balcony overlooking the lake. She snagged a fresh cup of champagne in passing, downed it, then set the empty glass on a serving tray.

She needed space. She needed to breathe and clear her head of all this nonsense. Being disconnected from reality didn't look well on her. It clouded her judgment and kept her from focusing on what was truly important—not dancing and spending afternoons daydreaming on flowery riverbanks. Work. Life. Her career. That was what was important.

Maggie placed both hands firmly on the stone wall, inhaling deeply. She closed her eyes against the erratic breeze, hoping it would cool the fire burning in her chest.

"You're boat girl, right? From this afternoon." She turned toward the voice, and the gentleman who had offered help while she was in the water stood beside her, sipping liquid amber from a lowball glass. He wore a scarf around his neck and a coordinating button-up vest, with dark skinny jeans and black lace-up boots. Well put together, slick dark hair, and salt-and-pepper stubble lining his jaw. Very trendy, very modern. Very big city. "You look like you need this more than I do." He finished the drink in one swallow. "But unfortunately, I don't share well with others." He chuckled at his own joke.

"It's been an interesting day." She smiled at him.

"So?" he asked.

Her eyes narrowed, not sure what he was asking about.

"Did it float?"

The boat. She laughed lightly and said, "Oh yes. I've never seen a boat float as well as the ones made by Garrity Boatworks."

She sounded like an overly pushy radio commercial.

"I've been thinking about that boat all afternoon."

"Really?" Her eyebrow arched, and her brain started running in forty different directions.

"Yeah, absolutely. It looked wicked awesome. Quality craftsmanship."

She took that to mean *really great*. Gears began to turn in her mind. She could run with this. This could be the lead she needed to get Finn on board with expanding his business. It would be a good thing—he just didn't know it yet.

"But it's not something I would buy blindly. I'd need to take it for a test drive, just like I would before I bought a new car. To see if we mesh, you know?"

"I completely understand, Mr. umm... I don't believe I caught your name."

"Will Tyler," he replied, taking her outstretched hand to shake it. "I grew up next door to Abe and Mary. I spend most of my time in Boston now, but I couldn't miss this. They were practically my own grandparents when I was a kid."

"Do you spend a lot of time on the water, Mr. Tyler?" she asked, trying to get as much information out of him as possible to see if she could sell him that floating boat. If this Mr. Tyler liked Finn's boat enough to tell his circle about it, Finn could have an easy following in Boston.

He played with the ice cubes in his glass, swirling them around the bottom. "I try to," he sighed, "but work has me busy these days. There aren't many places to fish in Boston." He chuckled, then set the glass down on a nearby table.

"What do you do for work?"

"I'm the artistic director for the Boston Playhouse. While it's the job I've always wanted, it keeps me in the dark for far too long. It makes me miss home, so as soon as a show closes, I head here for a few days to decompress."

"I can see why. It's absolutely beautiful. It's nothing like

Los Angeles."

"Is that where you're from?"

"It's where my job is. I'm an event coordinator, but I mostly work with charities. I get the occasional celebrity here and there, but it's mostly so they can claim the massive deduction on their taxes." Maggie rolled her eyes and leaned back on the rock wall, turning around to people watch. She didn't have a reason why she was being so honest with a complete stranger, but it felt good to do so. She was tired of lying to everyone. It just wasn't her style. "What if I could arrange a test drive for you, Mr. Tyler? How far in advance would you need notice?"

"Well." He paused. "I head back to Boston in the morning, but I should have things up and running within the next few weeks. I should be able to get away for a day or two once rehearsals start. I'd love to make a day of it and see the boats and designs when I come back."

A few weeks. That was longer than she planned to stay in Maine. No matter how much this place grew on her, it wasn't her place. It was Finn's. She would love to do the work, but Maggie wasn't all that sure he would see it that way. She could potentially expand his business from one coast to the other. Branching out and creating a business plan would be a great apology for the mess she put him in. What better way to say *I'm sorry I almost ruined your life* than introducing the rest of the country to his incredible talent? Maybe she could stay an extra day...but it wouldn't be for *him*. No matter how much he wanted it to be. She needed to make this right the only way she knew how.

A spectacular event that would draw in only the best of clients. Hell, she knew enough people in the medical field to perhaps even get Tess some connections to help Colin.

There would be flowers. Billowing cloth-draped tents with pillows. Bubbly champagne, and fruit and cheese plates. That melted brie with a whiskey glaze to drizzle over strawberries and sliced apples. Hand-wrapped chocolate from a local patisserie, if she could find one. An intimate gathering, one couple per boat. It would need to be catered, and she'd need to hire and pay a staff, of course. It was such short notice. It would be a tall task, even with her persuasive skills, and putting something together clear across the country would prove difficult. Oh yes, she could do it. Her plate was already overflowing, but she could make this work.

She could maybe even raffle off a boat. Or hold a silent auction. With quick marketing and an elite guest list, but she could rally her connections all over the country. With her plan, perhaps this Will Tyler would buy two boats. Or a yacht. Did Finn make yachts? Come to think about it, she really didn't know *what* he built exactly. She hadn't taken the time to ask. Her entire trip had been about her.

"Here's my card," said Mr. Tyler, handing her the small piece of paper. Give my office a call next week and we'll set a date. A pleasure to meet you, Miss Maggie."

"Thank you," she replied, taking the card from him. It was sleek, and black with white and gold lettering. A crying mask wailed in the top right corner. She slid it in the back pocket of her jeans and excused herself. She had work to do.

She had to go home.

• • •

Finn found Maggie leaning against the stone balcony wall, overlooking the lake. The moon shone bright over the water, reflecting upward along the metal hulls of boats, mimicking the twinkling of the night stars. The loons greeted him with their evening calls, the eerie, wavering tremolo sounding his presence. A gust of wind whipped her hair in wild circles, and she brought her hand up in an attempt to tame it, but kept her gaze focused on the water. He took a step forward, but stopped, unsure of what he needed to say.

Maybe he'd already said too much.

Or maybe his honesty was just what she needed.

Hell, he didn't even know himself.

He blew a long breath through pursed lips and rubbed at the tension building in his nape and shoulders. Had he pushed her too far? His honesty had scared her, but his words had been truth. Was he overthinking Operation: Win Back the Bride? Words were not the solution to show her how wonderful life together in Rockport could be. Maggie had to come to that conclusion herself. He just needed to present her with the right opportunities to do so. It had all been going so well. Or maybe he'd been going about this all wrong.

Maybe it *had* been just a dare for *her*.

Self-doubt clouded his thoughts. Maggie was, and always would be, way out of his league. He would never be good enough for her. But, damn it, he would love to spend his life trying to be. He might not be a man of position, but hell if he couldn't give her the love she deserved. If only she would see what he felt for her—still felt for her even after all this time— give him one chance to show her a glimpse of her future with him. Could he give her the life she didn't know she wanted, or was his life too simple?

He straightened. It was now or never, and it was getting late.

She turned against the wind slightly, and she caught a glimpse of him, making her turn fully to face him.

"Hey," he said, stuffing his hands into his pockets.

She wrapped her arms around her middle against the chill. "Hey."

He opened his mouth to speak, although had no idea what to say, when Maggie spoke first.

"Do you think we can go home? It looks like it might

rain, and it's really cold out here. Sorry I disappeared. I was having a great conversation and I didn't realize I'd been MIA for that long."

He chuckled. Maybe he really *had* been overthinking it. "Sure." He pulled the keys from his pocket. She wanted to go *home*. To his house. *Their* home. "You wanna drive?"

"You're lucky you're cute."

"So…that's a no?"

She lightly shoved his shoulder as she walked past. "Melinda's *your* prison bitch now."

"You're freezing. Where's that hoodie of mine you stole?" He caught up with her within a few strides as they circled the house and gardens to the front of the property.

"In the Jeep," she told him. "And I didn't steal it, I commandeered it. That's what boat people do, right?"

"I think you're thinking of pirates. There's the Jeep." He gestured up the drive into the darkness.

She paused. "I can see my breath." She huffed heavily into the night air. "I don't know if it ever gets this cold in California."

Gravel crunched beneath his feet when he came to a stop beside her. He took one of her hands in his, wrapping his palm solidly around it. "Yeah, but do your stars look like that?" He pointed up toward the heavens, the night sky amassed with the brightest splattering of constellations he'd ever seen.

Her hand cautiously slipped around his, steadying herself, taking his attention from the sky. "It's so beautiful. I could stare at this all night," she said.

He watched her, standing there with her head tilted back staring up at the great expanse, her eyes full of momentary wonder. A soft smile curled the corner of his mouth. "Me too."

Chapter Thirteen

Maggie dropped her purse on the couch, a vocal sigh filling the room when she spotted her phone still sitting on the table where she'd left it. She slipped it into her back pocket. "My feet are killing me." She twirled a lock of hair between her fingers and brought it to her nose. "And I smell like…fish poo." Her face wrinkled in a disgusted scowl. "I need a shower. Do you mind if I shower first?" She headed for the stairs. "I ran into Mr. Tyler at the party tonight," she told Finn.

"I don't know who that is," he said, following her.

"The guy from the lake this afternoon. He runs a theater." She grabbed a fresh towel from the linen closet in the hallway and tucked it under her arm. Then she removed one shoe, took a few steps, removed the other, and left them where they fell as she made her way to the bathroom. She wriggled out of her top, letting it fall to the floor as she walked and talked. "You've never met him before? He grew up near Abe's place. Lives in Boston now."

He collected Maggie's trail of garments as he walked behind her. "Oh yeah?"

She shimmied out of her bottoms and turned on the water in the shower. "Oh, thanks, I was gonna get that," she said as Finn dumped her belongings in a corner of the bathroom.

He sat down on the closed toilet seat. With her bra and undies still on, she stepped into the far side of the tub and closed the curtain. Once sure she was covered, she unclasped her bra, held it outside the curtain for a moment, waiting for Finn to take it. When she felt the tug from her finger, she did the same with her undies. The warm water rushing over her was a welcome relief. She ached in places she didn't know she had muscle groups.

After soaking her hair, she popped her head around the curtain. "He likes your boat." She held out her palm and wiggled her fingers at him. "Shampoo?"

Finn looked around the bathroom for a moment, then found her cosmetic bag and dug through it until he found the travel size bottle of shampoo. He placed it in her outstretched hand.

"He's interested in buying one," she continued, disappearing back behind the curtain. She squirted a dollop of the floral-scented shampoo onto her fingers, then passed the bottle back.

"I can add him to the wait list," he told her, his inflection changing to that of interest instead of placation.

"Uh-huh." Once her hair had a good lather, she rinsed, then opened the curtain again. "Conditioner."

He rifled through the bag once more, found the bottle, and handed it over. After taking what she needed, she gave him back the bottle and ran her fingers through her hair. She wished she could tell him of her plan. Tell him of all the wonderful ideas she had for him and his family, and his business. But she couldn't. Not yet. Not until she had it perfected.

Maggie swallowed hard. Her thoughts drifted back

to their conversation at Abe's. She wanted to tell Finn she would stay, wanted to make him happy, but she couldn't. She was only going to break his heart. But how to tell him whirled into muddled thoughts. Her body and her mind were at war. She'd felt so at home over the course of the day. And now, he was sitting in the bathroom with nothing but a shower curtain between them, and it seemed so *normal*. So right. And the realization of that scared her. Her brain melted into a puddle of mush.

She quickly finished up her shower, continuing to tell Finn more about her conversation with Mr. Tyler and his interest in his boat. She shut off the water, and he passed her the towel without her having to ask for it. She wrapped it around her torso, whipped back the curtain, and stepped out of the shower.

A muffled ring sounded from somewhere within her pile of clothing on the bathroom floor. "Shoot," she said, trying to navigate the tiny space. "I probably have a hundred voicemails by now." Although not having to worry about work had been a welcome respite.

"Here, let me help," he offered, standing and moving closer to the door. "I think it's coming from—"

"It's in my pants, I think." Maggie scooted by Finn, nearly face-to-face, body against body. With one hand holding her towel precariously around the important parts and one rifling through the pile, she reluctantly answered her phone.

"Hello?" She shot up, nearly headbutting Finn in the jaw. It was her father. *Shit.*

"Margaret?" It wasn't so much a question as it was a yelling declaration. "What the hell is going on? Where are you? I've been calling you. I've called every hotel and bed-and-breakfast in the area, and no one has you checked in."

She pulled the phone away from her ear slightly before turning down the volume. He was absolutely yelling. The one person she purposefully never called back.

Finn cringed. "Sorry."

She waved him off. Her dad's attitude wasn't Finn's fault. It was her fault she'd left her phone in the house all day. "Hi, Daddy," she told him, trying to play it cool.

"I haven't talked to you in days. What is going on? Have you fixed your little problem yet?"

"I'm working on it. And speaking of working, I wanted to ask you if—"

"Get it done. Tomorrow," he snapped, cutting her off.

"It's a bit more complicated than that," she told him, opening the bathroom door to pace the hallway. She'd been called to help here. It's what she did. It was the fuel for her fire, burning deep in her soul. Why didn't he get that?

"I don't want to hear your excuses, Maggie. I'm tired of dealing with your inconvenient mess-ups. The clock is ticking. And we still have a wedding to plan."

God, she wished she could reach through the phone and slap the stupid out of him. "There's not going to be a wedding. Winston and I are done. We broke up. The only reason we were engaged in the first place was because it's what *you* wanted. I have an opportunity to do some work here, and I'm staying until it's finished. Because that's what *I* want to do." She didn't know where the sudden burst of defiance came from, but she liked it. Miss Independent had her groove back.

She needed to stop apologizing for his behavior. "I am not going to be your puppet anymore. I am my own woman and *I* will choose who I love and who I'm going to marry. I am so sick and tired of everyone telling me what to do. You, Winston. I'm done with it all," she said with surety. "I don't know when I'll be back." A complete lie. She knew exactly when she was going home, but he didn't need to know that. He no longer had a say in her life.

There was silence on the other end, and Maggie glanced

at her screen to make sure the call was still connected. Her father cleared his throat, but he still didn't speak. She continued her pacing, not going to be the first to speak. She wouldn't crack. She couldn't. This was *her* life. She was in control, and he needed to be reminded of that.

The silence between them was deafening. Little drops of sweat beaded at her hairline, and she brushed them away with the back of her palm. She inhaled sharply, ready to talk, but he spoke before she broke.

"Stop acting like a child. Get those papers signed and get your ass on the next plane home. Do I need to remind you what's at risk if you don't follow through with this marriage?" He seemed overly calm, as if he'd been reading from prompts. "No wedding, no Kelley-Fisher Wing, no more funding your stupid head-in-the-clouds ideas."

Was he serious?

Did he think this was just some game? A prize to dangle in front of her?

She could bitch it right back. She didn't need Winston or his family money.

After a deep breath she added, "Divorces take time, Daddy. Despite what you might think, they don't work on your timeline. I'll be back, but it won't be because you told me to. It's because I have projects to finish, and I intend to see them through."

"That's a good girl, Margaret."

Gag. That voice. Like he was calling over a playful puppy. It disgusted her. "*No.* I'm not your good girl. I am a grown woman. I'm not Winston's arm candy or his trophy-wife-to-be. I'm not his anything, and I don't have to put up with being treated this way." Her connections in California were solid, and if he wanted a fight, well, he had one. "Don't call me again about this." She ended the call. *Damn you and your selfish ultimatums.*

She was done. She clutched the phone in her hand, banging it against her forehead in frustration. The tether had been severed.

"Too soon for an awkward pickup line?"

Maggie groaned. How embarrassing for that to go down in front of Finn, especially after what had happened at the party. Embarrassing, yet…exciting. She smiled. Was this how she was supposed to feel? Happy? Elated? Over the moon? Her motivation had just been thrown into overdrive.

And she was standing in the middle of her husband's hallway, wearing only a towel.

Her father's call had thrown her back into a stark reality. She had so much work to do, and she needed to stop playing around. The day had been wonderful—she couldn't remember the last time she'd been so carefree and happy—but California was waiting for her.

"I'm sorry," he muttered, running his fingers through those beach-boy waves. "That didn't sound too good."

"This isn't your fault. This needed to happen. A long time ago. Don't be sorry for me, be excited." She bounced on her toes slightly. "Be happy for me. This is awesome. I can finally do things my way. I am so sick of being told what to do, where to go, who to talk to. I have always been little Maggie, the people pleaser. Did you know the only way I could get my parents to notice me was if my achievements made it to the paper? Then they could show it off to all their friends at the yacht club. Proof I was worth something." She adjusted her towel. "State of California spelling bee finalist and my parents didn't even show up. Sent my nanny. They had more important places to be. I am my own person, damn it. And *I* make the decisions. I can't wait to get home. There's so much work I can do without all the bureaucracy and damned red tape at every turn. I don't have to ask anyone for permission to be *me*."

"That must have really sucked."

"You don't realize how lucky you are. Your family is amazing. They love you unconditionally, and that is a rare quality."

"They love you, too." He leaned against the wall, turning his head in her direction.

"They love the idea of me. Let's keep it real." She tightened her grip on her towel, then ducked into her bedroom to dress. With a nagging burden off her shoulders, she slipped the engagement ring from her finger. Her hand felt light without it. Free. No longer in chains. She crossed the room and tucked the diamond away in her suitcase. No longer would she worry about disappointing people who had no say in her life.

· · ·

Finn quietly closed the bathroom door. He shook slightly, flexing his palms. She really *was* available. And so damn strong. Her dad on the phone was yelling so loud he could hear the entire conversation, and, like a pro, she told him how it was going to be. A normal person would have crumbled under that sort of pressure. He'd love to see her in action— her authoritative voice was kind of a turn-on. He blasted the water for a shower and waited for the hot water.

And waited.

He sighed. *Cold shower it is.* He stripped, braced himself, and stepped under the steady stream of icy water. A small grunt left his mouth on a breath, and he showered as quickly as he possibly could, but it still didn't clear the image of Maggie in a towel just inches from him. He dried off, pulled on a pair of gym shorts, and headed to his room.

He couldn't stop thinking about what Maggie had told him about her childhood. A part of him wanted to make sure she'd never feel that way again. He paused in front of her bedroom door for a moment, then knocked. The door immediately swung open.

"Hey," she greeted, smiling briefly before slackening her mouth into a luscious pout.

He stood there for a moment, unsure of what to say. He didn't think she would open the door that quickly, or at all. His stomach rumbled, and he blurted, "Midnight snack?"

She brushed the hair from her forehead, raking her fingers through her hair, doing that *Little Mermaid* thing again, driving him wild. "I could eat something sweet."

He'd devour that sweet mouth had the timing been right, but right now what she needed from him was comfort and conversation. Thankfully, he had a half gallon of chocolate chip cookie dough ice cream in the freezer, and he hoped that would do. "Ice cream? Straight out of the carton?"

"Works for me!" She closed the door behind her.

In the kitchen, he grabbed two spoons from the utensil drawer and the ice cream from the freezer, and plopped down in a chair at the table. He slid a spoon over to Maggie, who sat in the chair beside him.

"Oh, the good stuff," she said, popping the top off the ice cream container.

"So tell me about this hospital thing you're doing," he said, taking a scoop of the ice cream. "Something for kids?"

Her eyes lit up. "I am so excited for this project." Her smile faded then, and she took a bite of the ice cream. "It's probably nothing you're interested in. I won't bore you with the details."

"No," he replied. "Tell me about it. What you were telling my dad seemed really cool. I'm interested, Maggie."

She swallowed and then licked the remainder from the spoon. "Okay. Well—I saw a need for a family wing on the oncology floor of the hospital my dad works at, so I'm fixing it.

Families were paying out the nose for hotel rooms while their children were receiving treatment, and I figured they could all use a place to stay, free of charge. Having to figure out how to pay to be with their children shouldn't be something else they have to worry about. They're going through enough as it is. So... I'm putting together a gala to raise the construction costs to get it built. It's going to be a separate building on the hospital campus. Housing and treatment at the same location. Rooms that look like home, not scary hospital places with tubes and wires everywhere. I've never done a project this big before, and I'm really starting to wonder if I'll be able to pull it off."

Her look of uncertainty tugged at his heart. "Do you work remotely a lot, doing all these things? I imagine the schedule is pretty busy."

She took another bite. "No, not really. I mean, I am right now because I have to. I like being there for every step of everything I do, because each project is important to me. I want to be there when they break ground. I want to see their faces when we cut the ribbon. I need to be at this gala. I need to make sure I do all I can to get the funding for this. Without Winston backing me now, it's going to be much harder. I just don't move in the same circles he does, you know?"

He understood. Her job was just as meaningful and hands-on as his was. He took another bite, letting the cream melt over his tongue. His mind raced in too many directions. He might not have the connections her ex could've given her in L.A., but there were other things he could give her. Respect. Commitment.

Love.

"Whatcha thinking?" she asked, breaking his thoughts.

He shook his head and sighed slightly, leaning back in his chair. "Nothing." He swallowed, then cleared his throat. "Maggie, I..." He sighed. "For the record, I would have gone to your spelling bee. I never would have missed it."

The corner of her mouth turned upward. "Thanks. But I know that's not what's bothering you, Finn. Tell me," she pressed.

"Okay." He swallowed. Truth time. "I don't even know the guy, but I don't like him. I don't like the way he treated you. I don't like how he's kept you from your dreams." He scratched at the hair on his jawline. "I'm jealous of the guy and I hate his guts. You're not even engaged anymore, and he's still controlling you. I don't like it."

"I was introduced to Winston at some function my parents were hosting. They told me this was the man I was going to marry, and I, being the people pleaser, went along with it. Be quiet, look pretty. Smile and nod. I think I was more than he bargained for, honestly. Can I confess something to you?"

"Absolutely."

"When I found out we were still married, I— I got that rush all over again. Vegas was still fuzzy, but I remembered how you made me feel. And I knew I was never going to get that from Winston. I had no idea what to expect when I got on the plane to come here. I was so nervous I threw up in the bathroom before I boarded."

He slid his palm across the tabletop, settling on hers. He squeezed. "Maggie—"

"I like who I am when I'm with you. Is that crazy?" she asked.

"No." Not when he felt the same.

"I feel like we've known each other our entire lives. It's so strange." She sighed.

"Listen. I know you keep saying you need to get back to California, but I will never ask you to leave. I love having you here. I love who I am when I'm with you, too."

She gave him a weak smile, squeezed his hand briefly, then broke the connection. "Enough about me. What about you? Is work going well?"

"Work is great. Aside from the fact that I haven't been doing much lately because, well…" He smirked. He'd much rather be spending every second he could with her. "I have a waiting list with deposits that will take me into the next five years. It's nothing as heroic as what you do, but it keeps me busy. I love what I do. I love creating these single, one-of-a-kind masterpieces."

"I'm not heroic."

"You are to the family of the kid in the hospital." Finn placed his spoon on the table and looked her in the eye. "Maggie, you have absolutely no idea how amazing you are, do you?"

"Since you have so many orders, why don't you look into expanding—"

And there it was. The moment he'd been hoping to avoid. Have *the talk* about Garrity Boatworks. "Look." He cut her off, setting his spoon on the table with purpose. What he was about to say was going to cut, but he had to lay it out there. He wasn't going to pacify her like Winston did. "I know it's your nature to help. That's what you are—you're a helper. And I *love* that about you. But, and I say this with the utmost sincerity and flattery—Garrity Boatworks doesn't need help. It's doing just fine here in Rockport."

"There's so much potential out there. You can hire employees. Take orders and keep a regular schedule. Branch out. Boston. New York. Even as far south as Savannah. Not to mention all the resort areas like Cancun and the Caribbean. You're so talented, and I want the world to see that. You're limiting your potential by staying local. Just imagine what you could do with this in California."

For a moment, being together in California crossed his mind. Dropping everything to be together. But rationality consumed him. "I don't need to expand. The way I build boats, I..." His voice wavered. "It's a very specific skill I don't want to market. I want to pass it down to my son, just like my father did to me, and his father before him." Her heart was in the right place, but he could never have someone else building boats with his name on them if he couldn't see them himself—to make sure every beam, every angle, was perfection. He loved building. He took pride in every boat. Garrity Boatworks was the only legacy he'd leave behind. "Thank you, really, but it's not something I'm willing to do."

She blew the hair from her face, her mouth twisting into a frown. "I understand."

"Besides, you seem to have a full plate already."

She tucked her knees up under her chin and hugged them. "Okay. So you don't want to branch out. What if you did something locally? I've been thinking a lot about this, and I want to put on an event for you. Showcase your work. What you do is such beautiful artistry, and it deserves to be appreciated. You yourself said it's been here for generations— let me remind the people of the gem they're overlooking. I really screwed you over, and I want to make it up to you. And this is the only way I know how."

He sighed, sinking back into his chair. He didn't need help. He didn't need to be thanked. He didn't need some event. He didn't need to branch out. But that look of desire in Maggie's eyes had him questioning everything.

What he really needed was her. He had no idea what something like whatever she had planned would cost him, but going along with whatever schemes Maggie had in that smart brain of hers might mean she'd stick around longer. Sticking around meant more time to finish Operation: Win Back the Bride.

This could be something they could work on together. Be together. Persuade her into staying longer, and longer. With him. "Garrity Boatworks has been in Rockport and Rockport only, and that's how it's going to stay. But, if you want to plan some event that would get the community together, I'm not going to say no. If it's something you want to do, I'll support you one hundred—"

Maggie sprung from her chair. In an instant, she was on him, squeezing him tight. She squealed, and he pulled her in close, embracing her frame.

"All right," he whispered in her ear. "Do your thing." He closed his eyes, content to just breathe her in. She smelled of soap and shampoo and everything right in the world. When she began to pull back, he groaned, "Let me guess. You already have a theme picked out?"

"I do." She seemed absolutely giddy with excitement. "This is amazing. Thank you for letting me make up for the annulment paper thing that I still say you were supposed to take care of."

"Oh, we're never going to live that down, are we?"

"There's so much to do."

He stifled a yawn. "I need to sleep."

"I'm going to get a head start, and get these ideas down while they're still fresh. We'll talk in the morning?"

"Whatever you want." He gently kissed the top of her head, allowing himself to relish in the sweetness of her being. "Sweet dreams, Mags."

Chapter Fourteen

There would be no sleep for Maggie. Not tonight. Not while she was buzzing with so much happy. She pulled her hair up into a ponytail and found her reading glasses in case her eyes grew tired. With her laptop in front of her and her planner at her side, she was ready. Her fingers clicked away, typing all her ideas. After it looked like something from a textbook, she titled it in a swirly font: Sunset Sail. It was perfect.

Maybe it was the delicious smell of brewing coffee, or most likely the dripping pile of her own drool on her forearm that woke her with a jolt. She snapped to attention, wiping her mouth with her hand and straightening the black frames on her face. She blinked away the sleep, her eyes focusing on the screen in front of her. A solid twelve pages of *aaaaaaaaaaaaaaaaaaaaa* screamed back at her. She flipped the lid of her laptop closed.

"Mornin'." Finn sat across the table with a cup to his lips and both elbows on the table. He raised an eyebrow.

She groaned. "How long have you been sitting there?"

"You talk in your sleep," he said, gulping from his cup.

She stretched the tingle out of her arms. "Creeper."

"By the look of things down here, it was a rough night, and I'm still not sure who won the fight. You want coffee?"

"God, yes." She rubbed the knot taking up residence on the back of her neck. Every inch of her ached. She hadn't planned on sleeping at the table, for sure. "Your crappy internet won that fight," she told him, rummaging through the stack of papers she'd resorted to using because she couldn't get her online software to open.

Well, it looks like you got a lot done. How late did you stay up?"

"I stopped keeping track after I almost threw my laptop out the window." Still groggy with lack of sleep, she attempted a half-hearted sorting to make heads or tails of her notes. She remembered writing key points in the margins from the night before. She'd written the profit margins in the margins— because it had been funny. At four in the morning. Now, not so much.

"So. How girly you making this thing?"

"It's not..." Lost in her thoughts, her voice drifted in between the rustling of paper. "Hold on, let me find the paper I'm looking for." She stuck her pen in her mouth and pulled out a ripped piece of notebook paper. "Got it. I know you said you wanted to keep it local, but I have this *fantastic* idea to show potential buyers your work, right here in Rockport. It will take some time to put together, but if I can get my people here from L.A. and my nonprofits, I could probably even get you some doctors who specialize in spine and nerve injuries. They could help Colin. It would be too easy to strike up a conversation with them and see if we can't get him in to see a world-renowned specialist pro bono. It's worth a shot, right?" She glanced up at him. "I'll need to borrow your blanket fort."

Confusion settled on his brow. "You need to what, now?"

She straightened in her seat, pushed her glasses farther up on her nose, and scooted her chair closer to Finn's. "Just *shhh* for five seconds."

"Such attitude, Red," he sassed back. "I like it."

Maggie glared at him, blowing an errant lock of hair that eluded capture by the hair tie from her eyes. "Excuse me?"

"This"—he drew a circle in the air around her profile—"so hot."

She smacked his arm.

"Very naughty librarian."

"I'm trying to be serious here." She covered his mouth with her hand. Wet, squishy, icky tickled the inside of her palm and she withdrew her hand. Had he just licked her? *Eww.* She rolled her eyes and wiped the spit off on his shirt. "Look. I need you to trust me," she blurted, thrusting her notes to him across the table. "Please. Just let me do my thing. You're giving me my divorce, and you deserve this." Time to make him see that she could truly help. And that she wanted to. He really deserved it. It was the least she could do for barging back into his life and turning everything upside down on him. "Let me make this up to you." Their eyes connected, and she waited.

He swallowed and licked his lips.

Then slowly took a sip from his cup.

The suspense was killing her.

Watching the way his lips moved was killing her—the way they glistened after running the tip of his tongue over them made concentration seem impossible.

She loved her idea, and the best part was they were able to plan it together. She couldn't remember a time when she'd been this excited to put together a project. "What do we do first?"

"*That* is a very good question," he said. "I need to go run some errands today. Do you want to tag along? Play tourist?

I need to go downtown, and I have some parts I need to pick up."

"Hmm," she hummed, opening cupboards until she found a mug, then poured herself a cup. She really needed to finish up her work. She was so behind on *everything*.

"Jo's coffee shop is downtown."

She paused. Bribery. He was bribing her with *good* coffee. And it totally worked. She placed the still-full mug on the counter and replied, "Can I shower first?"

. . .

Finn's errands were nothing special. A few stops for Nana, and the grommets he'd special-ordered were finally in at the hardware store. In truth, he just wanted to be near Maggie. Just being in her presence filled his heart. She made him want to be better. Do better. Who he was when he was with her felt good. He was happy, damn it. And when she came trotting down the stairs wearing his hoodie, it took all he had not to scoop her up in his arms and kiss her right then and there. Every fiber of his being begged him to make a move, but the thought of it pushing her away held him back. His mind and body waged war. He sucked in a breath, hoping she wouldn't notice just how badly he needed to adjust himself. "I'm never getting that back, am I?" he told her, happy to see her wide grin.

"Nope. It's mine now." She grabbed her purse from the table beside the front door.

She climbed up into his Jeep like a pro. He paused for a moment to admire the way her jeans hugged her ass before rounding the vehicle, climbing in himself, and cranking the engine to a roar. No blasting music this time—instead he enjoyed the analytical conversation Maggie started on whether or not there was a direct relation between the lift in a truck and the size of the owner's penis when a massive truck cut them off at an intersection.

The first stop was Jo's, as promised. It was busy with a line practically out the door, but Maggie seemed content to wait with him, making small talk about how chilly the morning air was. He rubbed his palms up her arms in an attempt to warm her, then wrapped her in a bear hug, swallowing her frame into his. He buried his nose in her hair, committing the smell to memory. Hints of cocoa and vanilla clouded his senses.

He was still holding her when Jo recognized them in line. He watched her falter, compose herself in a fraction of a second, then smile. "Hey, you two!" Jo greeted. "How's it going?"

"Hey, Jo," he said, reluctantly unwrapping himself from Maggie.

"The usual?" she asked, grabbing a cup from a stack near the register.

He nodded. "Please."

"What'll you have, Maggie?"

"Vanilla latte, please."

"Milk or soy?"

Jo never asked that, ever. She took her coffee seriously, and most times it was her way or the highway when it came down to how her specialty drinks were created. She was taking Maggie being vegetarian into consideration, and his insides warmed.

"Milk, please, thank you for asking."

"Coming right up!"

Jo busied herself making their drinks and Finn pulled his wallet from his back pocket. When Jo shook her head at him, saying it was on the house, he stuck the cash in the tip jar instead. Two steaming cups appeared on the counter and he grabbed them, mouthing *thank you* to Jo. For the coffee. For not making it weird.

They exited the shop, stepping out into picturesque Small Town, America. They stood together against the aged brick wall of the coffee shop for a moment while Maggie blew on her coffee, taking small sips of the too-hot liquid in silence. Antique shops and little cafés lined the storefronts of towering old three-story buildings that had stood the test of time. Townsfolk greeted one another as they passed by with friendly smiles and hearty waves. In the distance, gulls circled in the sky over a departing fishing boat. So serene. And so perfect.

"Why didn't you tell me she was your ex?" asked Maggie in between sips. "Before baseball?"

He started toward the hardware store. "I didn't think it mattered."

"She's really sweet." Maggie interlocked her arm with his. "Do you think it bothers her that I'm, well, she thinks I'm your fiancée? She told me about how she left, at Tess's house the other night. About how you two broke up. I think she regrets it."

"Oh, she knows about Vegas. I told her everything when I got back. About meeting you, getting married, all of it." How he'd made the biggest mistake of his life giving up so easily.

She stopped walking.

"I don't think I need to outright ask her, but I'm pretty sure she can put two and two together that we're still married."

"This whole time?" Her eyes were wild with shock and radiant wonderment at the revelation. "She knew I was acting the entire time and didn't say a word."

"She's really good at keeping secrets."

"So she said."

"You jealous?"

"I might be!" She playfully swatted his bicep.

"She's the one who convinced me to go to California a couple months after Vegas."

The color drained from her cheeks. "You came to California?"

"Yeah." He shrugged as if it were no big deal while taking a gulp of his still-too-hot coffee. "She knew how upset I was and told me to grow some balls and just go find you."

Her gaze softened, her mouth slackening. "So why didn't you?"

He pushed himself off the wall, avoiding her question. "The store is just up here."

"Answer me, Finn." She tugged at his arm, stopping him. "Why didn't you come find me?"

He touched her cheek softly, rubbing a curl between his thumb and finger. "I did. I showed up at your doorstep and was met by your father. I'm really surprised he didn't shoot me on the steps. He gave me this whole speech about how I was going to ruin your future and your potential. I was just a carpenter, would never be held to your standard. I was just some rebellious fling she had with the boy on the other side of the tracks, and somehow, he made me believe it all. He even tried to pay me off to shut me up. I said some not-so-nice words to your dad, tucked my tail between my legs, and left."

Her eyes flitted about. "You came back for me," she whispered. "All this time, we could have..." Her voice trailed off, and she stepped away from him, lost in her thoughts. "Had I known—" She looked up at him then, sadness enveloping her gaze. Her lips were slightly parted, and she looked as though she wanted to speak but had forgotten how to form the words. He'd seen that look before, on himself. Pure regret.

"I'm so sorry, Finn. I didn't know. I wish—"

"Don't." He pulled her close, taking her hand in his. "It's water under the bridge. I have regrets, too, Maggie. The store is just up here." He changed the subject, and they continued walking a bit farther down the main thoroughfare of Rockport until they reached the hardware store, where Finn collected his sail grommets. He introduced Maggie to some friends, and they finished their coffees while perusing the aisles of trinkets and touristy items, like postcards of the harbor puffins and miniature lobster trap keychains.

Finn then took Maggie through a labyrinth of stores ranging from the bank to make a deposit for Nana and an antique store beside a local art gallery to a food truck at the wharf that served black bean burgers for a late lunch. Maggie's smile was worth choking one down.

The sun had begun its descent by the time he'd finished his list, and he'd let the daylight get away from him. While Maggie was looking at necklaces made from sea glass, he checked his phone to see what time sunset was. He still had some time to get her to the perfect place to see the sun meet the water. "Hey, you ready? I've got something to show you, but if we're going to catch it, we need to get going now."

"Okay," she replied, exiting the shop with him. "Where are we going?"

"You'll see."

"If this requires me getting soaked again, I'm going to have to pass."

"You're going to like this one. I promise," he told her, walking with hastened steps toward the parked Jeep. They drove a few miles down the coast through a neighboring town, stopping on the side of a road near a narrow walking path through the woods. He took her hand in his, leading her closer to the most pristine bit of ocean beach he knew of. A peninsula of weathered rocks, accessible only during low tide, jettied out into the water, revealing a spectacular western view. The tide was already out, making the short climb onto the rocks more manageable. Eventually, Finn found his spot. It was a rock that formed the perfect high-backed bench, and the best place to watch the sun set on the water. The sky was splashed with vivid pinks and oranges when they finally settled down into their seat at the highest point of the rocky coast. A buoy bell rang somewhere on its perch in the choppy waters offshore.

Maggie leaned her head on his shoulder and exhaled. "It's stunning," she breathed, snuggling in closer. "The way the colors bounce off the sails. It's like a kaleidoscope on the ocean. I could watch this every night, and it would never get old."

"Today was a great day."

"It was. I had so much fun with you in town."

"See that one right there?" he asked, pointing to a boat bobbing against the waves. "I built that."

"Really? That's amazing."

They were quiet for a while, both taking in the colors and the sky as they slowly melded into the horizon. Finn pulled her in when she tucked her head closer to his chest, running his fingers lazily through her hair.

She framed her fingers around the boat, capturing the sunset inside them as if she were taking a photograph. "This is what I want to show the world. This beauty. I call it the Sunset Sail. The event, I mean," she continued, "and I think I got the theme just right."

"Hit the nail on the head with that one."

"I *am* jealous," she suddenly blurted out. She stiffened slightly, bringing her eyes up to meet his in the waning light. "The way Jo looked at us this morning, the way you were holding me. I could tell it bothered her a bit. I wanted to *be* that fiancée. And knowing that she knows all about our history, I was jealous she had you first. I just feel awful about it. I... I know what I came here for, but now... She's going to see what she's missing out on and try to rekindle things with you, and I just can't bear to even think of it. So yeah, jealous." She brushed the hair from her face. "Stupidly, ragingly, hormonally jealous." She exhaled sharply.

He kissed her then, soft and slow—no second-guessing. He wasn't going to allow another opportunity to pass him by, either. "I married *you*, Maggie."

She laced her fingers along his nape. "What are you doing to me?"

"What do you mean?"

"I come here with the intention of getting a divorce from this guy I met in Vegas, and now—" She choked, turning her head up toward the sky as if she would burst into tears if she continued. "Finn, I love who I am when I'm with you." She sucked in a breath. "You make this too easy, and that scares me. I can't believe I'm even telling you this."

"I'm glad you are, because I feel the same. You're a warm blanket on a winter's night, and I want nothing more than to lie in bed with you wrapped around me. How's that for crazy?"

She chuckled at that, but it was the truth. She made his house feel like a home. He hated to break the moment, but what little light they had left was disappearing at a rapid rate, and the tide was coming in just as fast. If they were going to make it off the rocks without getting wet, they had to go.

The drive back to the house was consumed by Operation: Win Back the Bride. His big plan had taken an unexpected turn when he wasn't looking, but maybe that was the point. Maybe if he just stopped trying so hard to make things work, the pieces would fall into place on their own.

• • •

Although crawling into bed seemed like the perfect solution for the rest of her night, the muffled banging, thumping, and sawing from the back of the house was far too tempting to ignore. After rising from the bed, she slipped on a pair of sandals and made her way outside and around to the back of the house. Two very large wooden doors stood between her and the noise. Should she bother him? Maggie bit the corner of her mouth in contemplation. Sure, why the hell not?

The door groaned as she pulled it open enough to slip through.

"Finn?" she called out. Birds on the rafters took flight at the sound of her voice, exiting the barn through an open set of shutters near the roof. When he didn't answer, she wandered farther in to explore. It had been a stable in its heyday, with remnants of stalls along the walls and a hayloft above her. But at some point, it had been converted into a workshop, with two very large, half-constructed boats in the center with tools and wood stacked on every workbench and shelf and shoved in every cranny.

A faded canvas hung loosely over the frame of one of his projects. A fine layer of sawdust had settled on it, seemingly abandoned and forgotten, except for a freshly cleaned section slung lazily over the back end. She approached it and placed a hand delicately on the canvas. It gave way under her touch, slipping to the floor.

Maggie forgot how to breathe.

She shook her head and refused to believe what her eyes saw. There, in faded white paint, was the name *Maggie Rose* scrawled on the beams. She blinked away the hot tears burning in the corners of her eyes. This was it. This was *the boat*. Finn had thrown everything he and Maggie had together into crafting it. It even looked like her. Wood stained a deep red, with flecks of a sparkling blue twisting and swirling as if the wind itself had painted it. It exuded happiness and warmth, with an electric energy and such...love.

But it had all stopped. It sat unfinished—unloved. Seeing such a talent left to waste away shattered her heart. She traced the fluid lines of the painted letters, the grain rough against her hand. He'd followed her, and she'd broken *his* heart—the unfinished pieces of it staring back at her in his work.

"Why did you marry me, Maggie?" His voice was gritty and dripped with raw vulnerability.

She whipped around to face him.

He stood just out of reach with arms splayed gently to his sides. Sweat and sawdust glistened on his skin and thin lines of wet dampened his shirt where it clung against the curves of his chest.

"It was the first thing I ever did for myself," she whispered to him. Her honesty hit her in the gut. Her only taste of freedom had been with him. Free to make her own choices and to love unequivocally, even in the most profound ways.

"Love" was a strong word. But so was "forever."

She stepped forward. The harsh light made the edges of his face sharp and distorted, and she found herself reaching up to brush away the hard shadow from his chin with the tips of her fingers. He caught them with his own and held them for a moment, pressing them against the angle of his jaw. The hair there prickled the tender skin of her wrist and she pulled back slightly, unsure as to why she'd done that in the first place. "I'd never pushed boundaries like that before, and in that brief moment in time, it was what *I* wanted."

"Is it what you want now?" His hands tangled in her hair, and he pulled her in against him.

A wild heat rushed through her and she pressed her palms weakly to his chest, making no true effort to stop him. She'd already melted into that heat, into his fervency, and whatever little effort she should put into rationalizing the situation disappeared when his lips found hers. He parted them with his tongue, tasting and taking.

She couldn't get close enough. Even though his arms surrounded her, she needed more. Maggie brought her mouth to his, taking his bottom lip between hers, and briefly sucked, then nibbled, before letting go.

He groaned deep in his throat before grabbing fistfuls of her bottom. His tongue found the pulse of her neck and he licked it, sending her arching against him. "I want a do-over, Maggie," he whispered against her skin, his breath hot against the coolness of her sweat. "I want you in my life."

The blurred lines of right and wrong—sex and sin—waged war inside her. Once more, she found herself free to choose, and she chose him. Finn.

She tugged at the hem of his shirt with a desperate need, clenching her fists in the material. Her thumbs hooked under the waistband of those Calvin Kleins, dragging them downward, inching closer to the vee of his hips. The vee she wanted to devour with her mouth.

"Maggie." Her name washed over her mouth when he kissed her. Deeply, fully, desperately.

She grasped at him, his arms, his hands, floundering in her need to touch him. All of him. Leading him to the unfinished portion of the boat, she climbed in, tugging him in after her. It rocked slightly but held firm in its cradle, ready to bear the weight of their world. She softly kissed him, her lips drifting to the shell of his ear. "Love me, Finn," she told him.

Demanded.

Chapter Fifteen

Finn blinked the sleep from his eyes. He stretched as much as he could without disturbing the sleeping beauty sprawled across his chest. His left arm tingled up to his shoulder, and his stomach growled in a long, continuous rumble, but there was no way in hell he was moving until Maggie woke. He had her in his arms, and he wasn't going to miss a second of it.

The sheets threaded through their legs in a tangled mess, and the cool morning air bit at his feet and calves—a stark contrast to the searing sizzle where her skin touched his. Last night had been unbelievable. Probably the best ever. Maggie had attacked him in the shop with the most mind-blowing sex of his life *in* her boat. She'd carried it over to the couch in the house and then, somewhere around one in the morning, they'd crashed in his bed. But that was before she woke him up at two and then again somewhere between five and six. He'd lost track of time after that. He would be exhausted all day—that was pretty much a given—but he wasn't one to complain about being tired from too much sex. No such thing. Completely spent and drained, yes. But too tired for

Maggie? Never.

Making love to her was something he'd never tire of. Holding her in his arms, tasting every inch of her, he wanted that feeling every day for the rest of his life. He considered Operation: Win Back the Bride a success. He had plans for today—he wanted to take her someplace special. Show her a bit of his childhood.

Maggie arched, unfolding from him like a seasoned sex goddess still reveling in late-night conquests. She kicked herself free of the sheets and groaned. "I'm *starving*."

He chuckled. "I wonder why," he told her, gently finding her lips with his. He lingered there, not wanting to break away from such a high.

She wriggled in close, nuzzling in the crook of his arm and shoulder. "More sleep," she yawned.

"I think it's past noon." A shadow crept along the floor across the room, where the French doors to his balcony had been left open all night. Then the sun popped through the clouds, illuminating the room once again. "And I need to pee."

Maggie laughed. "Valid reason." She rolled away from him, and the shock from the loss of her warmth made his skin prickle. She sat up, turned toward him and said, "I'll go make...lunch. And coffee." Those lips, soft and ever so slightly swollen from the night before, parted his with another kiss, and when she walked away from the bed, with those hips swaying that ass... Damn, she did it on purpose. She slipped into one of his shirts and left him alone to fight the increasing urge to chase after her for an afternoon throwdown.

Sighing hard, Finn scratched his hardening junk, rolled out of the bed, and found a pair of clean shorts to throw on. After a pit stop in the bathroom, he rounded the corner to the stairs. He paused, leaning on the balcony railing to watch Maggie below. She was dancing around the kitchen to music he couldn't hear. When she reached for something in the cabinet above her, the shirt rose, teasing him with a glimpse of her curvy backside. God, she was beautiful. Fiery hair loosely piled on top of her head, the creamy skin of a shoulder peeking out from beneath the collar of the too-big shirt, and legs that were the stairway to heaven. Maggie was a selfless soul and a spirit that ran wild when unbridled. How did he get so lucky?

The smell of melted butter and coffee wafted its way up to him, and, unable to deny his hunger any longer, he bounded down the stairs. "Pancakes again?" he teased, coming up behind her while she poured batter into a frying pan. He wrapped his arms around her waist and kissed her neck. "Are pancakes the only thing you know how to cook?"

"They're Mickey pancakes!" She held up the pan to show him the iconic three circles bubbling away in melted butter. "Everyone loves Mickey pancakes."

"They look like boobies. Everyone loves boobies." Finn cupped Maggie's breasts and playfully squeezed. "Boob, boob, butt." He cupped each in sequence, matching the bubbling blobs in the pan. "Boobcakes."

Maggie squealed, twisting away from him.

Finn grabbed a hot one from the top of the stack near the stove and shoved the entire thing into his mouth. "Why do they call them *boobs* to begin with?" he contemplated while chewing the still-too-hot mouthful. "It's not like they're something to be sad about. *Boo*bies. Why not...*yay*bies?"

Maggie arched an eyebrow as she added more to the stack. "Yaybies, Finn?"

For the first time since she stepped foot in his workshop, the idea that this could actually work crossed his mind. Just being near her, in the warmth of her wake, it felt real. He was wanted. She could split her time between the two coasts, work remotely, if that's what it took. The separation would suck at times, but not having her in his life at all would be the epitome of all suckage. A small sacrifice to pay for the greater good.

"Super happy fun bags, then." Hell, she had him thinking that spending some time on the West Coast wouldn't be so bad. She'd need someone to cook for her. No one could survive off pancakes alone.

She tossed her head back in a full-bodied laugh and swatted at him with the spatula. He caught it mid-swing, ripping it from her grasp. He had almost managed to get a butt-cheek slap in, when a knock on the door interrupted their little game.

He peered out the window. Tess's truck was parked out front.

"Mmm," Maggie stuffed a piece of pancake in her mouth. "I need to go put some panties on."

"Such dirty words." He turned off the burner and stacked the pancakes on a plate while Maggie flew up the stairs. "I don't think Tess is gonna care that you're not wearing any underwear!" he shouted after her. He unlocked the door, swinging it wide open.

"She absolutely *does* care if your fiancée is or is not wearing underwear." Tess replied, pushing her way through the door. "There's no telling what you two have done on the furniture."

"Best to stay off the couch, then." He scrunched his face at Tess as she passed by.

"Ooh, breakfast for lunch. I dig it." Tess headed straight for the food.

He stretched his arms above his head and lazily followed. "Yeah, about that... *Might* wanna stay away from the table."

Tess froze mid-sit.

"And that corner counter over there, too." He sat beside her and nodded toward her seat. "I think that one is safe."

"Thank you," she articulated, rolling her eyes while dropping onto the chair. She grabbed a plate and stacked it high with pancakes.

"Hi, Tess!"

Finn and Tess turned toward the balcony at the sound of Maggie's voice. She'd changed out of his shirt and was fully clothed, which annoyed him for some reason. Tess eating all of his boobcakes annoyed him even more.

Maggie bounced down the stairs, barefoot and beautiful. Her hair was loose, glinting like the waves rushing to the shore during a summer sunset. He opened his mouth to speak but couldn't find words. God, she was perfect.

And *his*.

He returned her smile, his gaze following her to the table.

"Hey, Loverboy!" Tess snapped her fingers in his ear.

Finn turned quickly at the startle. "Yeah?"

"Did you hear anything of what I just said?"

"Nope."

"Maybe if you picked your chin up off the ground and stopped ogling her like she was a ribeye then you would have. I asked what you guys are up to today. Obviously not work, since you're eating pancakes past noon." She shoved another forkful of syrupy goodness into her mouth. "Hey, these look like Mickey Mouse," she added, swirling what was left of her last pancake in the syrup left on her plate.

Maggie sank into a seat across from Finn. "Hah, match point goes to the wife." She pointed a finger at him. "Told you! Boobcakes, my ass."

"Whoa, whoa, you aren't married yet. Let's go easy on the names, all right? It's weird enough already." Tess licked the back of her fork, then set it on her empty plate. Just like that, half of his boobcakes were gone.

"The state of Nevada says we are," Maggie mumbled, fixing herself a plate. "Finn, could you pass the syrup?" She looked up at him expectantly.

Eyes focused, mouth straight, he stared at her. Then slowly passed the jar of syrup across the table.

"What?" she asked, before her eyes grew wide in realization. "Oh shit." She covered her trembling lips with her fingers. Maggie glanced at Tess—who was sitting with her mouth agape and her eyes darting back and forth between them—then back at Finn. "I'm sorry."

"Will one of you tell me what the hell is going on? And the *truth*, this time?"

He sighed, sucking his teeth. "We're married, Tess." The words blurted out of his mouth in sweet relief. Saying those words *finally*, instantly made his chest feel lighter. It was bound to slip at some point, but this wasn't exactly how he'd planned on telling his sister about his ruse. No, this isn't how he'd imagined that conversation going at all. He'd planned on Maggie moving in first, for starters. Or, maybe not telling her at all. Why did anyone have to know about the first marriage anyway? They could have two anniversaries. But it was too late for all that. Maggie had spilled the beans, comfortable in her surroundings. Now it was truth time.

"When did this happen?"

He leaned forward on the table, resting on his elbows. "Oh, about eight years ago."

Tess breathed heavily from her nose. "I'm confused."

"Remember that bachelor party for Tommy the guys dragged me to? In Vegas?"

"Yeah, you were gone for like, a weekend. Like, four days, tops. Are you telling me..."

"We eloped in Vegas. On my twenty-first birthday, to be exact." Maggie cut in. "We ran into each other, and the rest is history."

Tess slapped the table with her palms. "I knew it! I knew all that girlfriend crap was made up! There was just no way."

She laughed, pulling her phone from her back pocket. "But married? Oh, this is just too good. I gotta tell Jo."

Finn put his hand on his sister's, lowering the phone. "She already knows, Tess, and she's kept that secret for the last eight years. I expect you to do the same."

Tess turned to Maggie. "So why are you here after all this time? Where have you been? Why have we never heard of you until now? And how do you explain that rock that's... missing from your hand?"

Maggie was quiet, sitting there with blushing cheeks and a pout he wanted to kiss until it turned into a smile. Truth kicked him in the balls. "To get a divorce," he answered, his voice quiet and low. "The ring isn't from me."

"Oh."

A numbing awkwardness settled over the room. He sighed deeply, attempting to make some sense of what had just happened. Tess now knew their truth. What she decided to do with that truth ate at him. They'd never been the closest of siblings, and they fought more than got along, but he hoped when it came down to it, she'd respect his wishes. He had his reasons, and he was sure Maggie had her own. The last thing he wanted was to ruin her, just like her father had predicted he would. He would not be that man.

Chapter Sixteen

Maggie stared at the ceiling in her bedroom and focused on how the tiny chips of peeling paint on the exposed wooden beams curled around the edges. They hung on until they could no longer carry the weight of the world on their shoulders and flaked off, one tiny chip at a time. If only life could be so easy—floating along until you landed in whatever spot you're supposed to spend the rest of your life.

Last night had been that easy. Last night had been Finn and free-bird Maggie and passion, and nothing else mattered. The world still turned without her. No phone calls, no meetings, no deadlines. All fun and games, and it had been glorious. Right up until the part where she called herself the wifey in front of Tess. She hadn't done it on purpose, and she hated that she'd revealed their secret. When Finn had told his sister the reason she was there, after all that time, she realized she hadn't even thought about the divorce papers. She'd been so caught up in his world that they hadn't crossed her mind. Not once.

Something had shifted.

A knock on the door interrupted her thoughts.

"Come on in, but only if you're ready for your Nana's hopes and dreams to be shattered."

The door cracked open and Finn popped his head in through the gap. "I'll take my chances." He smiled, wide and fake, in an obvious attempt to lighten the mood.

She buried her face in her hands. "Oh my God. I'm so embarrassed. I'm so sorry! I don't know what I was thinking." She sat up on the bed. "I *wasn't* thinking, that's my problem. I can't believe I told your sister that we're married!"

He stepped into the room. "Well, technically, I did, after your awesome foreshadowing. Figured I'd just go with it, at that point." He closed the door and leaned against it.

"What if she tells your Nana? Your dad?"

"It's fine. Stop being so hard on yourself. She won't. We had a talk before she left. I gave her the highlights, and she promised to keep her mouth shut. Not sure how long that'll last, but you're still Michelle, for now. She understands. And even if they did find out, it wouldn't be the end of the world. It would be a relief, actually."

He was so calm. Collected. Here she was, on the verge of tears, thinking she'd destroyed his family with her screw-up, and he was warming the room with his confidence. Tess's interrogation in the kitchen had brought her back to reality, but reality had changed. She found herself truly questioning if her plan was what she even wanted anymore. Finn had her questioning everything. Why was that such a bad thing?

Because it wasn't.

Staying in Rockport, forging a new path, grew more tempting by the day. He'd made her forget the pressures of California just by being Finn. *He* was how a partnership should work—respect, compromise, and not just a prop on someone's arm.

"What if I told you I had the magic cure-all that can turn

this entire day around? Would you trust me?"

"I'd say you're full of it."

"There's somewhere special I'd really love to take you. It's a pretty big chunk of my childhood I think only someone like you could truly appreciate."

She sat up, knees over the edge of the bed, letting her feet dangle just above the floor. She was intrigued. "Dress code?"

"Whatever you want. It isn't someplace fancy."

Her eyes narrowed. "Water or land?"

"Land," he replied, "but I'll never say no to getting out on the water. In fact, there's this lighthouse I'd love to take you out to see sometime. The best view is by boat. Big boat."

"One surprise at a time. I could really use the distraction."

"It's a plan, then. I'll meet you downstairs when you're ready." Finn gave her a curt nod, then left, closing the bedroom door behind him.

She slipped into her Louboutins and ran her fingers through her hair before loosely braiding it to the side. She kept her makeup neutral, as she had absolutely no idea where they were going, gave herself a once-over in the mirror hanging on the back of the door, and grabbed Finn's hoodie from the bed before heading downstairs.

"Hey, you ready?" she called, bouncing down the stairs.

Finn looked up from his work and smiled. "Wow," he replied, tossing his pen onto the table. He stood, pushing the chair back with his legs. "You look amazing."

"Thanks. You don't look so bad yourself." *Truth.* The way those jeans hugged his ass so perfectly had her seriously considering investing in a few pairs of the women's version for herself if they'd make hers look that scrumptious. The sleeves of his button-down shirt were rolled up to just above the elbows, accentuating those arms...the ones that had held her so tenderly the night before. The security she'd felt was strange and unlike anything she'd experienced before. It had felt like...*home.*

Finn grabbed the keys from the table near the front door and pointed to the hoodie Maggie clutched. "Are you seriously stealing that? It's my favorite one."

She shrugged and followed him out the door. "Maybe. I'll let you know. It's growing on me." She carefully pulled it over her head, then pushed her arms through the overly long sleeves while Finn locked up. She loved how the soft fabric inside brushed against her skin, so she wrapped her arms around her middle, relishing in the instant warmth of the sweatshirt. "You know, I don't think I even own one of these. This is my first hoodie."

He cocked his head, his eyes narrowing in on her failing attempt to hide a smile. "It looks better on you, anyway." He opened the passenger door of the Jeep for her.

"Thank you, Jeeves." She cracked a smile and climbed inside. "So, any chance you'll tell me where we're going? Just a hint?"

"Nope."

"Not even a little one?"

"You'll find out when we get there." He cranked the engine to a roar.

"You're no fun." She faked a pout.

"On the contrary, I find this lots of fun."

The drive took them northeast along the coastline thirty minutes from Rockport, over stunning coastal inlets and over ocean bridges with fishing boats below. Colorful buoys bobbed with the tide, and Finn pointed out various historical landmarks when they drove by, most of them connected with childhood stories of him and his buddies getting in some sort of trouble there. He was a fantastic storyteller, and Maggie found herself immersed and asking more about his childhood, where he grew up, and the antics his parents had to put up with during his younger adventurous years. She particularly loved the story he told her about how he and his cousin Ryan used to string Black Cat firecrackers between the guts of their G.I. Joe action figures and blow them to smithereens. For fun. It was a wonder he survived with all ten fingers and ten toes. She laughed until her sides hurt, wishing she'd been around to witness such epic childhood adventures.

The laughter settled into a quiet stillness when Finn pulled into an empty parking space at the Coastal Cancer Center. "This place and the people here became a second home to me when my mom was going through chemo," said Finn as he turned off the engine. "I thought you might like to meet my mom."

A punch in the gut. She inhaled, sucking in a breath so deep her lungs were nearly bursting, but it kept her eyes from welling. "I would love to meet your mom," she whispered, unbuckling. Maggie followed him through the front door, where the receptionist promptly greeting him with a loving smile and a hug.

"Finn," she fussed. "It's been too long. We're so glad to have you today. I hope you'll stay and visit for a while. Your mom's knitting corner is still going strong." The woman waved them to follow her through a side door. "Make yourselves at home," she told them, then returned to the front desk.

In a cozy living room setting were various treatment setups, with medical equipment, a corner play area for kids, and patients varying in ages in recliners hooked up to an array of machines and tubes. TVs playing movies adorned the walls, and a teenager was playing a car racing game on one near the back. Three people were involved in a very intense card game in the other half of the room. It instantly gave Maggie that homey feeling of comfort and warmth, and she ventured farther in with Finn.

He led her to a small nook near a large window. Two rocking chairs faced a beautiful garden blanketed with roses and wildflowers. Inside a wicker basket between the two rockers were skeins of colorful yarn with knitting needles poking through. On the wall was a framed picture of a woman sitting in a rocking chair, knitting a hat. Maggie recognized the smile—it had the same crooked upturn of the top lip as Finn's did.

"Is this your mom?" she asked.

"It is." He lightly kissed his fingers, then placed the kiss on her portrait. "She would knit hats every time she came in for treatment and give them to the patients to wear. For months. Pretty soon, she was teaching knitting classes in here, and hat production stepped up its game. At one point, she even had Dad and me knitting hats."

Maggie studied the details of his face, how his eyes swelled slightly with the remembrance of his mother. His full lips pulled downward into a slight frown. She wanted to run her thumb across them to wipe away his sadness. "She's beautiful."

"That she was." He smiled briefly, at an old memory, perhaps, then cleared his throat and moved on from the knitting nook. "I used to come and hang out with the patients, but life got in the way. You know how that is. But, I figured, seeing as this is your niche, I'd bring you on by."

She reached for his hand and squeezed. "Definitely the highlight of my day."

He squeezed back. "This place... It was a pivotal time in my life. We knew what Mom was going through was serious. But this place gave us hope, a sense of belonging, and a place to spend time together as a family. I really don't know if we would have had her with us as long as we did if it weren't for the people here. The extra time they gave us. I just wanted to tell you, your project? I get it. I understand your *why*." He shooed her with his hands. "Go on. Look around. Maybe it'll help you come up with some ideas for your hospital wing.

Talk to people. See what they want…what they need."

Maggie stood in the middle of the room, arms folded across her chest. Seeing it, taking it all in, was an inspiration. He was right. Her mind was churning out ideas faster than she could commit them to memory. The space was limited—small—but filled with warmth and smiles. She couldn't wait until she was able to see her own project spring to life. To be able to step foot inside it, put hands on her dream, actually see it through step-by-step. It was thrilling to imagine.

"I like your shoes," squeaked a voice.

Startled, she whirled around to face a cheery-eyed teenage girl playing on her cell phone. Her chemo drip slowly pumped away into the port under her shirt. She wore a light-purple-and-gray striped knitted hat and had a matching blanket on her lap.

"Hi!" She grabbed Finn by the hand and tugged him toward the voice. They pulled up nearby folding chairs and sat beside the girl. "And thank you. My name's Maggie, and this is Finn. What's your name?"

"Emily," she replied.

"It's very nice to meet you. Mind if we sit with you for a while? My…friend"—she paused, nodding her head toward Finn—"his mother was a patient here, and he wanted to show me around. I'd love to spend some time with someone who has great taste in shoes."

"She loves shoes more than me. It's a crushing blow." He winked at Emily and twitched the corner of his mouth up into a smile for Maggie.

She brushed the back of his hand with her fingertips.

He wove his fingers between hers and squeezed.

"I'm actually looking for shoes right now," Emily told her, flipping the cell phone she was holding so Maggie could see the screen. Various pairs and colors of heels flashed by. "I can't decide."

"What's the occasion?"

"Senior prom. Wanna see my dress?" Emily's sunken eyes lit up.

"Absolutely. Show me." Maggie scooted closer to Emily and squealed with her over how stunning the antique lace dress was, and how adorable her date would look in his tuxedo. Her heartstrings tore a little when Emily mentioned how her mother was searching for matching lace to raise the bodice a bit to cover her port.

"You're fierce. Don't feel like you need to cover up for them. You're beautiful." No child should have to think of those things. Emily should be worrying about what their first slow dance song would be and finding the perfect pair of shoes to accent that dress, not hiding the fact she had cancer.

"Did you go to prom, Finn?" asked Maggie.

His cheeks flushed. "I did"—he sighed—"and it was a disaster. "A buddy and I had this great idea that decking ourselves out in solid white top hats and tails was the best idea of the century."

"Oh no." Maggie cringed, shaking her head slightly.

"Yeah. I'm talking white cane and shoes. The whole nine yards, top to bottom. I'm not proud of that, and I hope I've destroyed most of the evidence."

"I'm sure your dad could produce a picture if I asked him," teased Maggie.

"Please don't."

"Oh, these are pretty." Emily clicked on a pair of dark-red heels.

"What size are you?" asked Maggie, clicking on the drop-down menu.

"Seven and a half, I think."

Maggie clicked on the size and the price popped up. Two hundred fifty dollars.

Emily sighed. "There's no way my mom can afford

those." She turned off the screen and placed the phone in her lap. Her once happy face turned sullen, and she turned her head to look out the windows. "She doesn't know I know this, but she struggles to pay for my treatments. I can't ask her to buy me fancy shoes. I don't know what I was thinking."

Maggie slipped out of her Louboutins. "These are a seven and a half. Why don't you try them on to make sure it's the size you need?"

"Okay." Emily removed her Converse sneakers and socks and carefully placed each of the delicate heels on her feet. They fit like they were made for her. For Cinderella. It was meant to be. "They're perfect," Emily gasped.

"And they're yours." Maggie gave the grinning girl a wide smile and wiggled her bare toes against the cool wooden floor. "I want a picture of you in your dress with your date. A full report. I'll leave my info at the front desk, and you'd better have the best night of your life, or else. Those shoes were made to make miracles happen, so enjoy them!"

"Thank you." Emily wiped at her eyes. "I don't know what to say. This is the nicest thing anyone has ever done for me. I'm never going to take them off." She paused. "Do you want mine? I mean, now you have no shoes!"

Maggie laughed. "No, it's okay. I have a pair of flip-flops in the car," she lied.

Emily marveled at her new shoes. "Thank you so much. Are you sure? These look very expensive."

"I'm positive. You are very welcome." They continued chatting and hugging until the girl's treatment was finished and her mom arrived to take her home. Emily proudly showed off her shoes, and her mother cried and hugged Maggie for minutes on end, which filled her happy meter to the brim.

"That was so special, what you did for her."

Finn had been quiet during their interaction with Emily. So much so that she'd begun to wonder if something was bothering him. She couldn't pinpoint it, but something had changed. "It's the least I could do. To me, those were my favorite pair of shoes. But to her, they were a reason to keep on fighting. It's fulfilling to have the means to bring others happiness. Even if it's as simple as a pair of shoes." She turned to face him. "You know?"

• • •

"Yeah. I know," Finn said softly. Just like how he knew his Operation: Win Back the Bride had come to an abrupt, screeching halt in his mother's knitting corner. Sitting there, watching Maggie interact with Emily so effortlessly, it hit him like he was running *heart first* into a brick wall. His mind and his heart were at war.

She reminded him *so* much of his mother. And the moment he'd realized that was the moment the world started crumbling around him. How could he keep a treasure like Maggie to himself? She was destined for great things. And him? He'd be lucky to be shaping wood the rest of his life. He gritted his teeth. Why? Why couldn't he be selfish? Just this once? They fit. She could have a future here. They could have a future together. What about that was so wrong? His insides twisted, and he wanted nothing more at that moment than to toss her into the Jeep and just...drive.

• • •

After saying goodbye to the staff and giving his mother's picture a little kiss, they headed back to the Jeep.

He opened the passenger-side door for her and offered her his hand. As she stepped up into the cab, his brow furrowed, and his mouth twitched to the side. "We need to find you some footwear. We can stop and grab you a pair somewhere. Want to get something to eat? I'm craving something. Not sure what yet, but I'm craving it."

She hooked her heels around his hips, pulling him closer. "I could eat." Her hands found his. Fingers threaded together, and she closed in around his waist. She was hungry. For him. His lips, slightly parted, hovered just above hers. "Thank you," she murmured against them. "For bringing me here."

"You're welcome," he breathed. "I hope I was able to show you some of the harder moments of my life, and that you were able to use that for the better."

"I would love to tell you all about my ideas over dinner. My brain is about to burst." She released his hands, only to find hers wrapping around the little curls at the base of his neck. She lingered there for a moment before pulling him in close for a kiss. She parted his lips with hers, tenderly, slowly.

Finn deepened the kiss, a soft groan escaping his mouth onto hers.

"About that dinner?" *She* wanted to be dinner, based on that kiss.

"This tastes pretty good to me." He chuckled, pressing his forehead against hers.

Maggie motioned toward the big bay window facing the parking lot and said, "Well, we'll probably be on the front page of the paper tomorrow if we keep this up. Someone just took a picture of us."

Finn stiffened and cleared his throat. "Time to go. I'm sure Nana already has the first issue. She's friends with the entire staff." He released Maggie and climbed into the driver's seat. "I know the perfect little place. I think you'll love it. It's right on the water, and it's going to be a gorgeous night." He smiled for a moment, then cranked the engine and backed out of the parking space.

Chapter Seventeen

Finn glanced at Maggie as he drove, lost in his thoughts and the music blaring from the speakers over the rush of the wind around them. His heart was heavy.

He found a parking spot on Main Street and they grabbed a cheap pair of sandals from a clothing shop, then headed along the sidewalk toward the water. Main Street was lined on both sides by connecting brick buildings with colorful awnings and swinging glass doors. It was all so very Rockwell and quintessential New England and exactly where he wanted to be. Rockport was like living in a painting, but without her by his side, it might as well be drained of color and light.

Signs with the day's specials interrupted their walk along with random racks of ocean-related souvenirs and bins of wooden toys in the shapes of starfish and shells. A wide array of aromas blasted them from all sides as the bistros and restaurants geared up for the evening dinner rush. His stomach grumbled in response, but he could no longer tell if it was because he was hungry or because he felt he was about to be sick.

When he led her into a quaint little chowder house on

the wharf, Maggie bounced on her toes in excitement. "This place is adorable."

"Adorable?" He rolled his eyes, then huffed a light grunt. "This place has the best steaks in town, despite its homage to soup."

"I'll let you be the judge of that," she replied, taking his outstretched hand. The hostess led them to a table next to a towering window facing the water.

It hadn't changed much since the day it was built, and the view couldn't be beat. Boats bobbed in the water as the sun made its descent to the horizon. He pulled out a chair for her, and, after pushing her in, sat across from her and took the menus from the hostess.

"The server will be right with you," she said with a smile before returning to the front.

Maggie cracked the paper menu. "Everything sounds delicious. Aren't you going to look at the menu?"

Finn, leaning backward in his chair, folded his arms behind his head and stared at the fishing boats tied to moorings in the harbor. "Nah." His eyes shifted to her. "I get the same thing every time I come here."

"Everything looks so tasty. I'm so hungry, I want everything on the menu. Maybe I'll let fate decide. It's gotten us this far." She closed her eyes, swirled her finger over the menu, then pressed it to a random spot. She cracked open an eyelid. "Oh! Their signature corn chowder. Fate must be on my side."

The cadence of her words turned his insides to mush. She was liquid to his solid. Words escaped him while caught in the depths of the waves crashing against his chest. She made it hard to breathe. When the waitress returned, he inhaled sharply, breaking the sucking emptiness growing in his chest.

"Are you ready to order?" the waitress asked, notepad in hand.

"I'll have the corn chowder and a coffee, please. Light

and sweet."

The waitress wrote on her paper. "And for you, sir?"

"I'll have a coke, the twelve-ounce prime rib with butter sauce—medium rare—double side of mash." He wasn't sure why he was ordering food. His appetite had left him as soon as they'd left the cancer center. What he needed to say to Maggie left him with a void he didn't know how to fill.

She cleared her throat and sat up straighter. "Okay. Are you ready for this? I want to get all these ideas out. Telling you gives me two memories instead of one, and I don't want to forget before we get back to the house." She practically bounced in the oversized wooden armchair as she proceeded to describe, in detail, the interior of her planned family wing for the center.

With elbows on the table, he dragged his palms down the length of his face. He wasn't listening to her anymore. Her words were drowned out by the erratic beating of his heart. The loud *thump thump* burst in his ears. He wiped sweaty palms on his thighs.

"You're a carpenter. Have you worked on building construction before? Or just boats? How are you with blueprints? I need to go over the final plans with the foreman here soon, but maybe you could have a look at them? Am I overthinking this? I know work is really jammed for you right now, but what do you think? Two first-class tickets? We could find an apartment somewhere. I can have Cara start looking tomorrow. We could even get a house cat." She paused, sucking in a breath. "Do you like cats? I feel like I'd like a cat. Maybe a rooftop garden."

He could only stare.

Her eyes widened. "Come to the gala with me. Be my date. We can get you a tux—and God knows how much I'd love to see you in a tux—and it'll be fabulous. Finn?" Her voice quieted. "What's wrong?"

"Maggie…" He pushed a breath through pursed lips. "You need to go back to California."

"I know, that's what I've been saying."

"Without me," he interrupted.

"What?"

"I need to get you on a plane. Your dream isn't ever going to happen unless you're there for every step of the way. That could take years. You are so hands-on, and motivated, and… You've been here less than one week, and you're planning cheese plates on my boats. I already have you forgetting what you really came here for. I'm just slowing you down."

His hands shook. He placed them in his lap. It had started out simple enough—showing her how wonderful life in Rockport could be—but instead she'd been showing him all along how it couldn't. He'd just chosen to ignore all the signs.

"Sitting in the Coastal Center with you and Emily made me realize you have this amazing gift, and I've been so selfish. It's something I can never fulfill, and it would be a disservice to those kids if you stayed here. I don't know why I didn't see it earlier. I guess it took being there, remembering what my mom went through, to figure it out. It dawned on me, watching you interact with the patients—I saw my mother in you. What she did while she was there, you're doing on a massive scale. She had the ability to help the community, but you? You have the opportunity to save lives. Those kids will have a chance at life because of you."

"I'm not a doctor. I'm just trying to get a building up."

"You know what I mean. You have the funds and the drive to get all those influential people with large checkbooks on board. The latest in technology, all that."

She twisted in her seat. "You don't know what you're saying. I can work remotely. We can split the time. We can make it work. Come with me. We can figure this out."

"I'm not going to California, Maggie."

Her eyes narrowed and her lips pursed slightly. "You've been trying to convince me to stay since I got here. And *now*, just when you actually have me thinking we can do this, you're kicking me out?"

"Tess can't do this on her own. Not with Colin to take care of. My duty is here, to my family. They need me *here*. The boats have been in my family for generations. It's in my blood. I can't walk away from that. There's no one else who can fill in for me when I'm gone. The shop has always been in Rockport, and Rockport is where it needs to stay. You've got to do this, Maggie." He reached across the table, gathering her hands in his. "You know I'm right."

She turned her eyes downward to their hands, clasped together for what seemed like ages. Then she whispered, "I know. It's just…"

He squeezed her hands, rubbing the pad of his thumb over hers. "It's okay," he whispered. "Look at me."

She opened her eyes.

"It's going to be okay. You finally have a chance to take charge of your life and do what *you* want to do. Don't let this place fool you into settling again. You have an entire building to build. Go kick some cancer ass."

She shook her head. "I'd just hoped… I don't know, I'd just hoped you'd change your mind. Being with you here has been wonderful. And I wanted us to be wonderful *there*, too."

"And your gala? As amazing as that may be for you, that's not me. You'll never get me in a tux, pretending to be someone I'm not, or in a room full of rich people who have nothing better to do than throw around money. All the fake faces acting like they'll remember me the next day. I'm not a city boy, no matter how much you'd like to change me. And I know you want to. It's in your nature to fix things. I don't want to be fixed."

He was throwing out truths faster than she could process

them. As hard as they were to hear, he was right. A small-town boy like him would be eaten alive in her world. He had saltwater in his veins. This ocean was his home. His life. His everything. No city could ever compete with that. It would lose, every time.

Her mouth was suddenly dry and she gulped her water, only to find it didn't quench her thirst. She had an overwhelming urge to flee and fought it back with every fiber of her being. She was being rejected for the greater good— this was a first for her.

A burst of air left her lungs, and she blinked furiously to keep the tears from falling. *Head up, chin up.* "So what do we do now?"

"Well, we have some great conversation over dinner, and tomorrow we'll figure the rest out."

"Figure the rest out?" She rolled her eyes. "The walls are crumbling, and you want to *figure it out*? When? In another eight years?"

"Come on, Mags. You know I'm right. You'd go crazy not being there for your project. Could you really leave that in the hands of strangers? Would they see your vision?"

She twisted her mouth, biting her bottom lip. "This is a hard pill to swallow, Finn, but I understand. I see where you're coming from, but this feels like Vegas all over again. A great weekend, no commitment, fantastic sex. I have my world and you have yours, and we're foolish to think we could ever combine the two. So we go our separate ways? Shake hands, good game?"

"It wasn't ever just sex for me, Maggie. I did that dare because I wanted to."

"Do you ever think about what would have happened if we *had* filed the paperwork in Vegas? Do you think fate would have brought us back together?"

"Would it have made a difference?"

A question she couldn't answer. She wiped away a tear and nodded. In agreement or in defeat—she couldn't tell. In finality, perhaps.

This was it. Whatever little thing they'd had was officially done. And it hadn't been her doing. He'd made the choice for her, and a little tiny fragment of her heart felt relief that she wasn't the one who had to make such a monumental decision. Like a lot of certainties in her life, it had been made for her. Only, this time, she was somehow at peace with it. He'd told her it was going to be okay, and it would be. She chose to believe him.

But that didn't mean it didn't feel like her world was collapsing and she was trapped under the rubble. Her mind couldn't comprehend the moment at hand, and she tried to focus on his words, his face. Instead, she closed her tear-filled eyes in a reluctant effort to break free from the pull he still had on her.

She *did* have to go home. To a home and a life that wouldn't have him in it.

Nor would it have her heart.

• • •

Finn tossed the wood planer onto his tool bench. *Hell.* He hadn't said a word to Maggie on the ride back to the house. He'd been scared he'd lose his courage and beg her to stay. He was doing the right thing. In his heart, he knew it was what was best for both of them. His mission had failed miserably. She was upstairs packing, and where was he? In the barn working on a boat with her name on it. A fantasy that was never going to play out. Relationships didn't just pick up where they'd left off eight years later. It hadn't even been a relationship. Did he seriously think over the course of a long weekend he could convince a woman he'd met eight years ago they should stay married and drop everything to be together?

He gripped the back of his neck and rubbed the tension building there. Getting his hands dirty had always cleared his mind, but for some reason, he couldn't get her out of his head this time. Every inch of the *Maggie Rose* reminded him of her. How the smooth edges felt under his hands and the adrenaline rush of completion. How his fists crumpled in her red waves and how he had tasted the salt of her skin on his lips in the very spot where he stood.

When he finally ventured upstairs, Maggie was in her room. He knocked lightly on the door. "Maggie?" No response. He balled his fist to knock once more but hesitated, placing his palm against the wood instead.

The door cracked open. "Hey."

He pushed it open wider and stepped into the room. "Packing?" he numbly asked, shaking his head, as the suitcase and items strewn over the bed made it obvious.

"I booked my ticket. Are you sure you won't come with me? I can easily change it to two."

"Mags." *Don't make this harder than it already is.*

She picked up his hoodie and scrunched it between her hands. "Will you promise to at least visit?" She held it out, filling the space between them.

"Keep it," he told her, knowing that the smell of her perfume lingering on it long after she was gone would break him into pieces. Of course he'd visit. When her wing was completed, he wouldn't miss seeing it firsthand. "What time is your flight?"

"Six a.m."

"Early."

"Yeah, well." She continued folding clothes and tucking them into her suitcase. "Any later and I might not get on the plane. I have so much to catch up on when I get home. The earlier the better."

"Want me to take you to the airport in the morning?" He leaned back against the wall, glad it was there to hold him upright. His legs felt like jelly.

She sighed. "I'm leaning toward no. As much as I'd like you to come with, the rental needs to be returned to the airport, and that would leave you stranded. And I think the drive would do me some good anyway."

"Well," he said, standing straight, "if you change your mind, I'm more than happy to take you. The drive could do me some good, too. I won't keep you." He took a step toward the door, then paused, turning to look at her. "Hey."

She turned to face him.

"I'm really proud of you."

Her cheeks flushed slightly. "Thanks."

"Night, Mags."

"I'll see you in the morning."

. . .

The alarm blared in his ears, disturbing his dreams. He awoke to darkness and the soothing patter of rain pittering on the roof. For a moment he lay there, lost in the foggy rift, caught between consciousness and dreaming, until the snooze alarm buzzed at him for a second time. Trepidation settled on his chest. He kicked the blankets back and stumbled out of bed, sliding on a pair of jeans and hitting the bathroom on his way downstairs. Maggie should be up by now, and most likely raiding the kitchen for her first hit of coffee for the day.

He descended to the first floor, the aroma of brewing beans curiously absent.

As was Maggie.

He stood alone in the dark. "Maggie?" he called out. He flicked on the kitchen light, illuminating the open space around him. The light glinted off the shiny cover of a notebook sitting neatly on the table. Beside it sat a handwritten note.

Finn,
You were right. I need to do this.
I'm sorry I didn't say goodbye.
I thought a clean break might not hurt as much.
The signed divorce papers are at the lawyer's office, when you're ready.
Wishing you nothing but the best in life.
I'll be seeing you.
Love,
Maggie

He opened the notebook. Scrawled inside on the front page was another note: *In case you decide to continue with the Sunset Sail.* Inside was the detailed event she'd concocted, neatly transcribed from her mess of scrap paper and diagrams. The date hit him in the face. June twenty-seventh. Maggie's birthday. Their Vegas Anniversary. Elvis day. Panic rooted itself deep in his gut. Her meticulous handwriting glared back at him in blue ink.

Shit.
Shit shit shit shit.

Maggie was gone. He wanted to puke. He sank down into a seat at the table, put his head down on his arms, and closed his eyes. *This was for the best*, he repeated, hoping one day he'd actually believe it.

Chapter Eighteen

Finn threw the broken board into the corner scrap pile. Another day wasted. He raised his eyes to the beams above him in an effort to keep his cool. Releasing a deep sigh, he brushed the sawdust from his hands and retrieved his beer from the workbench. It'd long grown warm but he downed it anyway, hoping it would help him to forget. He'd thrown himself into his work after Maggie left. Unsurprisingly, he'd accomplished very little, but he'd hoped working would occupy his thoughts. It did nothing to stanch the ache in his chest. Sleep eluded him, so he'd taken to losing himself in the wood and a few drinks.

So often, he'd almost pushed the call button. He had to talk himself down every time. He couldn't be a distraction. Maggie needed to focus on achieving her dream. He splashed his face with water from the mop sink and picked a new plank from the pile, starting over.

As he ran the board through the planer, the barn door to the shop opened, showering every corner with light. He squinted against the sudden change and cut the power to the machine.

"Jesus, Finn," said Tess, as she walked farther into the workshop. "How long have you been in here and… What is that *smell*?" She surveyed the room and then him, eyeing him up and down several times. "When is the last time you took a shower? Or shaved? You could put Viking braids in that thing." She pointed to the full beard he hadn't bothered to touch in…he didn't know how long.

"I don't know, Tess. What does it matter?" He set his board against the hull of the boat he'd been framing.

She eyed him with sympathetic eyes.

There was the *poor Finn* again. He didn't need her coddling. The whole reason he was staying at the shop was because he'd had enough of it from everyone. "What do you want?"

She adjusted her weight to one hip and crossed her arms. "It's been a month, Finn. You've been wallowing by yourself in here for a *month*."

"So?"

"Look, I'm not going to treat you like some wounded animal like Nana and Dad are." She hesitated for a moment. "Do you wanna talk about it?"

"No." His exasperation with his sister hit an all-time high. "There's nothing to talk about. I told her to go home, she left, end of story."

Tess grabbed the wooden stool in the corner and planted herself on it. "But it doesn't have to be. Have you called her? What would she think, seeing you in here? You're miserable. You can't even sketch well, and that's serious." She nodded toward his sketches, stained and crumpled, on the workbench next to where she was sitting.

His sister was right about one thing. He no longer found comfort in his work. He didn't question his decision to let Maggie go—it was the right thing to do. If he hadn't told her to go, would she be at the lake house right now…with him? Quietly suffering?

"The way I see it, you have three options here, and you need to pick one. *Now.* I hate seeing you like this. She may have been here based on a lie, but you were happy. Probably the happiest I've *ever* seen you."

"I'm fine." He crossed the workshop to the mini-fridge next to the office and grabbed a fresh beer. He unscrewed the cap and flicked it into the trash, then took a long gulp.

"This is not you. Look at you! You're a mess!" Tess rose from her seat and grabbed the bottle from his hand. "Do you think Maggie would want you behaving like this?"

"Don't!" he growled back.

She slapped his shoulder. "Don't you growl at me, brother. I'm the only one in the family who's going to be straight with you. You want the *poor me* act? You're not gonna get it from me. So here it is. One, you continue on this self-destructive path you're on, which doesn't do anyone any good. Two, you suck it up, buttercup. Go over to the lawyer's office, sign the documents, and move the hell on. Three, which is my favorite choice"—she pointed her finger in his face—"you get your ass in the shower, and then you get your ass on a plane and go get your *wife.*"

"It's not that easy."

She clucked her tongue. "Yes, it is."

"What? I'm just supposed to stop everything, leave you and Colin here, forget the shop, and just...go?"

"Well, *yeah.*"

He rolled his eyes. Like that could ever happen.

"The world will keep turning if you're not here, Finn. I love you, but I won't let you use me as your scapegoat. Colin and I will be just fine. What good is this shop going to do you if you can't even stand to look at it? How many more years is that boat with her name on it going to sit unfinished? Let me ask you this. Do you love her?"

He bit his bottom lip, running his fingers through his

tangled hair. *"Yeah."*

"Then that's all that matters. You're either going to live with her, or live without her. The choice is yours." She pulled her keys from her pocket. "Come on. Let me drive you home."

They didn't speak during the drive from the shop to his house. His thoughts were full of words. He replayed Tess's lecture, trying to make some sense out of everything. When they pulled up the drive, he slunk from the truck, muttering his thanks for bringing him home.

"Get some sleep," she told him through the driver's-side window. She shifted the truck into reverse. "And take a shower!" she called out, backing up.

Finn waved her off and dragged himself up the stairs to the front door. He pushed his key in, took a deep breath, then entered. Everything Maggie punched him in the face.

• • •

Finn woke not knowing what day it was. He stood in the shower trying to clear his mind until he ran out of hot water. As soon as the cold touched him, he told himself he needed to make a decision. And he did.

After changing into some fresh clothes, he grabbed his keys and headed into town. The harbor was tossing boats left and right as he drove by—a storm was brewing. He could feel it. How the air tingled the back of his neck and sparked at his fingertips when he touched his skin. The same as when Maggie touched him. He pulled his Jeep into an empty spot outside of the lawyer's office, hoping she was in. He ran his fingers through his hair, took a breath, and stepped outside into the hazy mist.

The receptionist, surprised to see him burst through the door, set her coffee down on the desk and wiped her mouth with a tissue. "Good morning," she smiled, eyes wide. "How can I help you?"

"I have divorce papers I need to sign with Ms. Richards. Is she available?"

"Let me go back and check. What is your name, sir?"

"Finnegan Garrity."

"Give me just a moment." The receptionist scooted out from behind her desk and disappeared behind a door with frosted glass.

He paced the lobby while he waited the longest wait of his life. The overwhelming urge to hurl twisted in his stomach, so he braced himself against the wall. He could make it back out the door in five steps.

"Mr. Garrity, good morning." Anna stepped out from behind the frosted door. "I have the documents drawn up if you'd like to go ahead and sign them." She motioned toward her office.

He followed her through the door while Anna spouted words and sentences he couldn't hear. She flipped pages before him, pointing to tiny lines marked with color-coded tabs, and he chuckled, thinking of how she and Maggie would get along well with their organizational skills. A pen was thrust into his hand.

"Mr. Garrity?"

"Hmm?" He looked up at expectant eyes.

"Sign here."

He pressed the tip of the pen against the crisp white paper. But no matter how hard he willed his hand to move, it wouldn't. He flipped through the papers, one by one, paying particular attention to each colored tab.

Maggie had never signed the papers.

Not a single one.

Fate was a funny thing.

He set the pen down on the desk. "Ms. Richards, thank you for your time."

"Mr. Garrity, is everything all right?"

"I have to go."

It was raining when he slid into his Jeep. He wiped the drops from his forehead and grabbed his cell from the cup holder. He dialed Tess. Straight to voicemail. He pounded out a text.

CALL ME.

He'd hashed this out in his brain a thousand times. He'd weighed the pros and cons. He'd resolved to go with the hand he'd been dealt and sign the papers. Whether or not this was some sign from the cosmos or something having to do with fate, he was running with it.

His cell rang halfway through his drive home. "Tess," he answered.

"Yeah?" her voice echoed through his sound system.

"I'm still married."

"What?"

"I went to the lawyer's office to sign the papers, but she never signed them. We're still married."

"Sooo... Did *you* sign them?"

"Nope."

"So..."

"Question for ya."

"Okay."

"How quickly can we find me a tux?"

"Have you finally cracked? Do I need to call someone?"

He laughed. "Nah, I just think fate is trying to tell me something. You're good with all that internet stuff. Can you do me a favor and see if you can find this gala Maggie was putting on in Los Angeles? It's a fundraiser for a kids' cancer wing. Look for Margaret Kelley. I'm sure there's probably something in the press about it. There're supposed to be a lot of famous people going. I'm not sure where, but I'm sure you could figure—"

"Got it," she interrupted. "It's in *two days*."

"And it's hers?"

"Yeah. I'm pretty sure. Her picture's on the website. Wow. Is she like, famous or something? This sponsor list is unbelievable. Royce Theater. Looks expensive."

"Focus, Tess." He pulled into his driveway. "I need to get there."

"Right. It looks like it's by invite only, and one of those 'buy a plate' type deals. Are you going to Mission: Impossible your way in?"

"I'll figure it out when I get there."

"Why are you going to dive-bomb her at the gala?"

"Because I know she'll be there. Any ideas?"

"Well, Jimmy over at Hitched owes me one. He mostly does wedding dresses now, but I can call him and see what he's got hanging out in the back. I'm sure there's got to be something in there you could wear."

He pulled the Jeep to a stop in front of the house. "Yes. Do that. I'm home now. I need to buy a plane ticket. Call me when you get something. Thanks, Tess."

"Have you showered yet?"

"*Bye, Tess.*" He spilled from the Jeep in his rush to get inside the house. He took the stairs two at a time, fumbled with the lock, then kicked his boots off on his way down to the kitchen. He searched flights on his phone while pacing the floor with a million thoughts racing through his mind. He found one that would get him to Los Angeles the afternoon of the gala, which was plenty of time. Plenty of time to pack, find a tux, get a haircut and a shave, and ask his dad if he could give Maggie his mom's ring. If fate was trying to tell him something, he was going to listen. There had to be a good reason that the papers were never signed. Did Maggie just... forget? On purpose? Just not remember?

If he was going to do this, he was going to do it right. All in. Double or nothing.

• • •

Finn checked his watch for the time again, even though he'd done it just thirty seconds before. His Uber was late. He exhaled and tugged at the tight collar restricting his neck. This was happening. He'd come to terms on some big decisions while on the flight. He touched the small box in the inside pocket of his suit coat, making sure it was still snug and secure.

His flight had landed at LAX right on time, and with no baggage to claim, his only priority was finding the Royce Theater and getting to Maggie. Every minute counted, and his driver was ten minutes behind and counting. The sheer volume of traffic buzzing by had him jumping in his skin. Taxis, buses, valets, and luggage everywhere. People running in every direction. Tearful goodbyes and cheerful hellos competing for curb time.

A small silver car pulled up, its lighted sign in the front window shining blue and bright. The passenger window shimmied down. "You Finn?"

He nodded.

"Sorry for being late, dude. Traffic has been insane today. I'm Jack." The driver was a middle-aged, balding man grinning from ear to ear.

Finn opened the back door and slid across the seat and buckled in. His knees pressed against the front seat, crumpling him into some sort of fetal position almost as badly as the planes had—all three of them. He was honestly surprised his tux had made it semi wrinkle-free this long.

"Looking good, my friend. You going to that big shindig over at the Royce, huh?" The driver made conversation as he pulled away from Arrivals toward the airport exit.

"Yeah."

"You performing or something? You look the band type."

That made Finn chuckle. He leaned against the window

to stare at the lights whizzing by. "No, no. Going to see about a girl."

"A girl, huh? Where you from?"

"Maine."

"She must be some girl."

He met Jack's eyes in the rearview mirror. "You ever made a stupid, stupid mistake and realized it too late, Jack?"

"I let a girl get away once. Biggest regret of my life. She went on and married some actor, had a couple kids, and now I get to see her on his arm whenever he's on TV. And here I am, single, alone, driving people around all day and night, lonely, and no girl to keep me warm at night." He sighed. "I wish you the best of luck, my friend," Jack said, pulling up to a towering building with a sweeping stone staircase out front. "We're here."

"Thanks." Finn opened the car door and slid toward the sidewalk.

"Go get your girl!" Jack shouted back with a send-off wave. "Don't forget to rate five stars!"

Finn bounded up the stairs two at a time. Several people dressed to impress straddled the stairs, chatting and smoking, paying him no attention.

"Excuse me, sir," said a raspy, very British voice as Finn reached for the door. Standing beside him was an older man with graying hair, dressed in full uniform, white gloves, and shiny black shoes. So shiny Finn could see his reflection in them as if he were staring in a mirror. Small in stature, but he puffed his chest with assertion anyway. The doorman stepped in between Finn and the door, eyeing him. "May I help you, sir?"

"I, uhh," he pointed toward the door. "I need to speak to someone in there."

"Do you have an invitation?"

"No, but I'm pretty sure she'd let me in."

The doorman cleared his throat while smoothing the front of his uniform. "This is an invitation-only event, sir."

The man seemed offended just by looking at him.

He could easily rush by the old man, make a scene, and most likely not be stopped, but he didn't want to push his luck. He sighed. "Have you ever—what's your name?"

"Alfred, sir."

"Of course, it is," he muttered. "Alfred, there's this girl inside, and I need to tell her how crazy I am about her. I came all the way out here just to tell her. The *grand gesture*, you know? Could you at least get a message to her? Let her know I'm out here and there's something very important I need to tell her?"

Alfred squinted and his mouth pressed into a frown. "How do I know you won't go inside while I go get this mystery woman?"

Because that's exactly what he was going to do. "Look, please just go get her. Her name is Margaret Kelley. Tell her Finn is here. I promise I will stand right in this exact spot and wait."

A couple scaled the stairs and passed a piece of paper to Alfred. He glanced at it, passed it back, and opened the door, motioning them through. "Enjoy your evening." He nodded. "Not you," he told Finn. Alfred looked about, then motioned Finn toward him. "You. Come here," he whispered.

Finn took a step next to him.

"Miss Maggie, you say?"

"Yes," he replied, a bit hesitant.

"Go and find your lady. I'm sure she'll be thrilled you've come all this way to see her, Mr. Finnegan Garrity." The purposeful punctation of his name was like a little needle stabbing him repeatedly in the eye.

Finn's stomach twisted and his heart beat fast in his throat. "How? Oh, you bastard." This whole time. This whole time, by the doorman. Well played, Batman's butler. Well played.

Alfred cleared his throat and opened the theater door.

Chapter Nineteen

Maggie fiddled with the loose bobby pin behind her ear. Peering down at the ballroom below her from the balcony of the Royce Theater, she noted that the event appeared to be going well. Only an hour into her gala, and she'd received many overwhelming compliments on the decor, her use of space, and the overall aura of the room, which calmed her nerves. Sort of. A year ago, snagging a Saturday evening at the Royce had been an impossible feat, but she'd overcome it with her fierce determination and inability to take no for an answer. Here she was, seeing it all come to fruition. The Royce was the pinnacle of Hollywood stardom in the fifties, and the old-glamour elegance still resonated throughout its halls. Its heyday had seen the likes of stars such as Grace Kelly and Marilyn Monroe. Such elegance once twirled in the very ballroom she watched over. And now, old millionaires put on a show for their friends. Who had the most money and means. Who could write the fattest check. The fakest of the fake.

Maggie didn't care. As long as it paid for a good deed in

the end, and pushed her farther toward what she set out to accomplish, that's what really mattered. Not the fancy cars or the one-of-a-kind dresses these women would never wear again. No, it was the people they would unknowingly help. The kids smiling through rounds of chemo. They mattered.

The catering waitstaff wandered the room below like little lost penguins in a sea of sparkles jetting back and forth on wave upon wave of silken fabrics. Glasses of champagne balanced on small trays covered with starched white linens. The orchestra played "The Blue Danube" in the corner of the ballroom, and it was perfect. Her gala was perfection. She'd done it. From start to almost-finish, she'd put together one of the season's most extravagant affairs. She'd even been interviewed by the senior editor for the *Los Angeles Business Tribune*. Full-on article with pictures. Seeing the write-up had been the single best thing that had happened since she had returned home. She'd put together her masterpiece on her own.

And she wished she had someone to share her excitement with.

This whole *living-your-best-life* thing wasn't all she'd hoped it would be. It'd been nearly a month since she'd left Rockport.

She had dived headfirst into her work, just as Finn had asked her to. She'd also moved out of her shared apartment with Winston the moment she'd arrived back in California. Thankfully, he'd already taken the initiative to have her things packed and waiting for her. Such a big help. It wasn't the new girlfriend who greeted her in the foyer, no. Not at all.

Maggie rolled her eyes. She was better off alone in her single-bedroom apartment. It was cozy, filled with plants she had managed to keep alive so far, and she'd even contemplated adopting a lap cat. At least, that's what she told herself at night when there wasn't any more work to be done and the only ones calling were Netflix and the pint of Chunky Monkey in the freezer. But even so, she still stood by her decision to leave that part of her life behind her. There was always a never-ending stream of events she could take on to keep her busy. Her so-called friends couldn't be bothered with her now that she and Winston weren't a thing. But it was okay.

She would be okay.

Everything would work out, and she needed to believe that.

Maggie smoothed the front of her gown. The sleek black fabric felt cool against her palm. She should really join her guests, but hiding out by the coat check with a glass of champagne was much more appealing. Her speech had gone over brilliantly, and the crowd had even given her a standing ovation. People had flooded her with excited compliments about her work and dedication. Smiled and clapped for her. Given her lots of money. She could be breaking ground sooner than she ever imagined.

She downed the rest of her glass and forced herself to rejoin the gala. People would start to ask where she was if she didn't come out of hiding soon. She placed her glass on an empty tray and wandered to the back of the balcony for one more once-over of the ballroom floor below.

Dinner was finishing up, and the round tables were being cleared to allow for dancing and socializing. Everything was falling into place beautifully. Cara, her assistant, was in charge of the cleanup crew, and it was the best delegation of duties to date. Staff payments were scheduled for autopay in the morning, cleanup would be finished tonight, and she didn't have to worry about a thing.

Until she saw him standing in the middle of the dance floor.

Sleek, fitted suit. Shiny black shoes. Bow tie folded just

so. Both hands casually resting in the pockets of the snuggest pair of trousers she'd seen in a long time, accentuating every curve and line of his body. *Every. Single. One.*

Finnegan Garrity was in a freakin' tuxedo.

In California.

Standing in the middle of her gala.

She braced herself on the railing.

The corner of his mouth twitched up into a half smile, and he sauntered forward. Cool, calm, collected.

Freakin' hot.

Maggie stood, frozen. Her feet were glued to the floor. Her lungs screamed at her to take in a breath. *Inhale. Exhale.*

Should she go down there?

She should go down there. If only her feet would listen to her brain and move.

You got this. One foot in front of the other.

On shaky legs, Maggie made her way down the sweeping grand staircase to the ballroom.

He swaggered toward her. "Hey."

"*Hhhhiii…*" she managed to squeak out as he got closer. And closer. And then his hand was on her lower back and she was spinning around the dance floor in his arms, and *was this real life right now*?

"You look positively radiant."

"What are you doing here?" she asked. A warmth washed over her. It rooted deep in her chest, spreading to the tips of her fingers and up to her cheeks, yet her skin prickled under his touch.

"Am I not able to support my wife on her big night?" he mouthed in her ear, his breath hot on her skin.

"We're not married anymore." A sudden sadness consumed her at the thought of no longer being his wife, even for the short time they had spent together. A large chapter of her life was over. That book was closed, and they had both moved on.

Or had they? Perhaps not, as he was still twirling her around the dance floor. She was in his arms, and in that instant, she knew there was no place she'd rather be. "Why are you here? Oh God, did I miss court? I hadn't heard back."

"I needed to tell you something."

"You crossed the country to tell me something? You couldn't call?"

The music slowed and so did Finn, whose thumb lightly traced the deep V-cut of her dress along the base of her spine. He laughed lightly. "Well, it's important. I figured I should probably tell you in person, and what better place than your gala?"

"And in a tux," she added, smiling. "Your beard." She lightly ran her fingers along the smooth, square lines of his jaw.

"It was time for a change." He took in a deep breath and held it, as if he was holding something back. "You never signed the papers, Maggie." He blew a breath out through pursed lips. His eyes flickered over hers, searching.

Her jaw slackened. "I..." Her thoughts scrambled to piece together her last few moments in Maine. She'd been so determined to get to the airport before she chickened out that she'd completely forgotten to stop at the lawyer's office. Maggie's weight shifted slightly, and she leaned in to him. "We're— "

"Still married," he finished. Finn stilled, breaking his hold on Maggie. He reached into the inside pocket of his jacket. "And I needed to give you this in person." He pulled out a slightly crumpled picture and passed it to her. "It's important that I do."

Maggie took it, running her fingers over the faces smiling back at her. It was Emily from the cancer center, clutching the arm of her prom date. She wore a stunning sleeveless gown adorned with bits of silver sparkle—port and all—and the Louboutins Maggie had given her. On the back of the photo was simply written, "Emily, Senior Prom" in looping cursive. She pressed the picture to her chest. Tears welled, clinging to the corner of her eyes, threatening to fall in mass numbers. Maggie blinked furiously in an attempt to keep them at bay.

This one little thing—the picture she held in her hands—was that simple, and that complicated. It wasn't the huge production or the name clout, just a little inconsequential trip to a treatment facility that changed everything. Changed her life.

It was the person. The story. The footprints left in the lives of others.

And it was all because of Finn. He'd taken the time to show her that no matter where she was, or who she was with, there was always an opportunity to help others. Even through something so small as giving someone a pair of shoes or a picture. Maggie looked up at Finn. "Thank you."

"You're welcome." He took her in his arms once more, his hands gliding over her with the lightest of touches.

Maggie pressed her head against his chest, still clutching the picture. She breathed him in, the salty air from an ocean away still clinging to him, and she closed her eyes, etching every movement into her memory. She may have tried to forget him in the month since she'd left him in the early morning hours, but her body hadn't, and it betrayed her. It ached for him, his hold on her only strengthening the need to be closer still. She licked her suddenly dry lips. "I know what I want, Finn."

He kissed the top of her head. "Yeah?"

"Yeah. I know that I have no idea what I want. I want to make it up as I go. I want a do-over." She smiled up at him.

He cocked an eyebrow. "Do ya now?"

She nodded. "I may not know what I want to do with my

life now that I've found out it's been a complete sham spurred by my parents, but my heart tells me no matter what I choose to do, I want you to be there. No matter what I dream at night, what avenues I explore now… There's been only one constant in them." Maggie placed her palm against his cheek, and he leaned slightly into it when she rubbed her thumb along his jawline. "You. I want nights under the stars. Adventures. Getting lost in the middle of nowhere. Road trips. An ocean, and it doesn't matter which one. I think you and I and the moon sounds about right."

Finn ran his fingers through the hair curling at his nape, all handsome and ruggedly wonderful. Mischief inched across his pursed lips. "This was supposed to be my big grand gesture, and I kind of feel like you're ruining it for me."

"What?" Her brow furrowed. She closed in on him, standing just inches from him, then rose to her tippy-toes, searched the fire in his eyes, and told him bluntly, "I'm trying to be serious here. I want a do-over." Maggie tucked the picture back into his pocket and wrapped her fingers around his palms, pulling him in even closer. She entwined her fingers between his. "Marry me, Finn. Again."

"The first time didn't do it for ya?"

"Shh," she hushed him. "I'm proposing here."

"I can see that." As much as he tried to hide his smile, it formed, lighting up his face and her whole world. "So am I." He dropped to one knee. He pulled the delicate blue box from his inside pocket. "Marry me." His mouth twitched. "Again." He opened the box, revealing the most stunning diamond-encrusted ring she'd ever seen. Oh, how it sparkled, just like when the sun kissed the peaks of the ocean waves.

"Oh my God." Her hands flew to her mouth. "*OhmyGodohmyGod.*" She focused on the starburst of green circling his irises, then on the dusting of tiny freckles along the indents of his cheeks.

"Mags?" He shifted his weight. "Everyone is staring," he whispered.

She hadn't noticed when the music stopped, nor had she realized the crowd had parted to the edges of the room and Finn and she were the only two left on the dance floor.

He cleared his throat. "When you showed up at my door, being with you again, I thought—I thought maybe it was my second chance. And then when you were gone, I realized I couldn't lose you again. I don't care where we live. I just want to be where you are. I've put the shop up for sale. I'll stay here with you in California, if that's what it takes to be near you. Maggie, please say you'll marry me."

"But you love that shop!"

He took her hand in his. "I love you enough to let it go."

She squeezed, pulling him upward to her lips. "And I love you enough not to let you." She wrapped her arms around his neck and clutched him close. Her tears soaked into the fabric of his coat.

Finn cupped her cheeks, his thumbs wiping her tears from her skin. "*You* are my ocean, and… I *love* you."

"Say it again," she whispered.

He narrowed his eyes. "The whole thing?"

"Just the 'I love you' part," she laughed.

"I love you, Maggie."

A shout from the balcony echoed throughout the room. "Hurry up and tell him *yes* already!" From the balcony, Cara threw her hands up in exaggerated frustration.

"Yes. *Yes.*" Maggie wiped the steady stream of tears from her cheeks, giggling. "You've ruined my makeup."

He slipped the ring onto her finger. "It was my mom's," he told her. "And now it's yours." He swooped her into a dip and kissed her as the music picked up, surrounding them with their own personal soundtrack. In the fleeting moment, she wondered if the night was just a very vivid dream sequence incited by a movie left on while she slept. It couldn't be real. Such perfection didn't exist, she thought, until the strings started to hum their song.

God, it was real. The kiss was real, Finn was real, and it wasn't just the champagne talking. "I love you," she told him, the surety of her words calming her jitters. "But I want to do this right. No Elvis, just friends, family—"

"And *cake*." Finn looked at her expectantly.

Maggie nodded. "Oh, there will be cake. Lots and lots of *cake*." Hell yes, there would be cake. Cake in the bedroom, cake in the shop. Cake on the kitchen counter. Even cake in that death trap of a Jeep.

Finn brushed the hair back from her face. He brought his mouth to hers, stopping just short of a kiss. "Maggie Rose Garrity," he whispered against her lips. "Is that a dare?"

A teasing smile curved her mouth into a devilish grin. "Oh, you have no idea."

Epilogue

Maggie triple-checked her planner. Her Sunset Sail was moving right along without a hitch. A fantastic display of Finn's work lined the dock, ready to disembark with the couples who had reserved them for the ride over to Blanket Fort Island. The caterers, the waitstaff, the musicians... Everyone was prepped and ready to go. All she needed were the guests. And Tess, who wasn't answering her phone.

Boats filled and disembarked for the island as townspeople meandered down to the lake, eager to showcase Finn's outstanding talent. Her contacts from New York, Boston, and even some from California had made good on their word, and Finn had personally rowed them over to the island. Even Mr. Tyler from Boston had brought an entourage with him. Everything was falling perfectly into place. With such an overwhelming response from the New England community, orders for custom crafts would be falling into Finn's lap by the weekend.

When the last few guests pushed off from the dock, Finn returned, towing a tarp-covered boat on a trailer. He backed it up into the water, then pulled the tarp off, revealing the most stunning work of art she'd ever seen.

The *Maggie Rose.*

"You finished it," she gasped.

"I couldn't let my girl show up to her Sunset Sail in a borrowed boat, could I?" Once he had it in the water and tied to the dock, he parked his Jeep, then returned to Maggie with a bouquet of wildflowers wrapped in satin ribbon. "These are for you."

"Thank you, they're beautiful." She planted a kiss on his lips. "I still can't believe you went through with this. How did you get everyone back on board after I cancelled?"

"That answer I'm taking to the grave," he chuckled.

"Wanna see if she floats?" Maggie asked him, pointing to the boat.

"After you, darlin'." He untied from the dock and pushed off. The *Maggie Rose* cut through the water with little effort.

She ran her fingers over the fancy, hand-carved etchings along the inside of the hull.

To Maggie from Finn, who never stopped loving her

Her heart leaped from her chest right into her throat. "Finn," she croaked. "It's perfect."

He smiled, continuing to row quietly across the lake.

They made small talk during the short ride, and Finn's one-word answers unsettled her. "Are you okay?" she asked him.

"Yeah." He continued to row. Beads of sweat gathered on his brow.

She wanted to believe him, but his nervousness upset her stomach. The night had gone perfectly so far, and she was worried something was about to go terribly wrong. "Are you having a heart attack right now? I can hear your heart pounding over here." When they rounded the bend to where he'd built a temporary dock on the island, everything suddenly made sense.

Soft lights lit up the walking path. Opaque fabric panels billowed overhead. People lined the walkway three and four heads deep. Even his Nana was there, holding a...veil? What was going on? Finn took her arm in his, leading her to Nana, who smiled and kissed Maggie's cheek. The antique lace veil was placed on Maggie before their walk down the aisle continued.

Flowers, check. Veil, check. Handsome groom, check. She was getting married. Again. Her knees buckled as a band played a soft wedding march in the background. Familiar friends waved to her from the crowd. She spied Jo hanging off the arm of a rather dashing man and gave her friend a quick thumbs-up. Even Edythe from the diner was there, clapping in the background with more townspeople Maggie hadn't had the chance to meet yet. They were all there. For them.

Next to Nana stood Tess, who smiled uncontrollably. Little Colin threw rose petals from his wheelchair from the front row as Maggie stood between family and friends.

"Mahalo," said a familiar voice from the end of the isle. Kai, in all his Hawaiian glory, grinned back at them. "I'd give you both leis, but Finn said he was the one who wanted to do the laying."

"See? I told you we'd have babies in no time! I'd say in about nine months!" Nana cackled to those standing nearby.

"Nana. Eww." Tess scrunched up her nose.

Maggie dabbed at her eyes, hoping her mascara was as waterproof as the packaging claimed it to be. Overwhelmed, she let out a cry that morphed into a hysterical laugh. "Did you plan all of this?" She beamed at Finn—her husband. Her future.

"I did. *I do.* Maggie, the love of my life. Today, in front of the many witnesses here, I promise you this." He took her hands in his. "I promise to never let you forget this day, like you did the first wedding. I'll never let you live that one down." Finn gave her a subtle wink, and the crowd chuckled. "I promise to support your unhealthy coffee addiction. I promise to love you unconditionally, even when you ruin my *favorite* classic rock songs by singing *way* out of tune. I promise to agree to disagree that your pancakes look like boobs. But most of all, I promise to never *ever* feed you veggie-con bacon again for as long as we both shall live. If you, you know, wanna."

Maggie placed her palm over his heart. Its erratic beat matched her own. "I promise to always kiss you good morning and goodnight. I know what love is because of you. And I promise you, some things are worth doing twice. And yeah… Hell yeah, I wanna."

. . .

Eighteen months later

Maggie sighed softly, content to soak up the summer sun on her rooftop garden. Golden beams filtered through leafy palms, splashing shadows over the bench Finn and she rested on. Her head lay in his lap while he lazily stroked her hair.

Finn glanced at his watch, then closed the book he'd been reading. "We need to get going."

"Mmm, ten more minutes," she groaned, covering her eyes with the back of her palm as the clouds moved, allowing the sun to poke through.

"Emily's flight lands in an hour. You should probably get there before she does." He chuckled, setting his book beside him. He placed his lips close to her belly and spoke softly. "Tell your momma it's time to go."

Maggie pulled her knees up. "You're horrible," she joked, placing her palms on her belly. "She just kicked me in the bladder, and now I have to pee."

He helped Maggie to a sitting position. "Good girl, Andersen."

She stood, arching her back and stretching out the kinks. "We've talked about this. We are *not* naming our daughter after sail rigging."

He grinned, grabbing his book. "I'll wear you down eventually, just give it time."

"Well, you've got about three months to figure it out."

"Plenty of time!" He slapped her backside lightly, then playfully darted through the door in front of her.

"You're lucky you're cute!" she shouted after him, following him through the door. She waddled down one set of stairs and one more door through the entrance to their California apartment. By the time she reached the bedroom, Finn was already shirtless and changing into a pair of fitted trousers for the ribbon cutting. She stopped to stare for a moment, wondering just how she got so lucky. If only she didn't feel like a beached whale.

Grabbing her dress from the hanger on her closet door, she undressed and slipped into it. "Can you zip me?" she asked Finn, unable to reach it herself.

"You look stunning." He kissed the delicate skin on her collarbone while pulling up the zipper.

Maggie gave herself a once-over in the wall mirror next to the closet. "Look what you did to me," she half-heartedly whined, adjusting the fabric over her baby bump.

"When a mommy and a daddy love each other very much—"

While hanging on to the bedframe for balance, she waved one shoe at him, then slipped it on her foot. "I should throw these at you."

"Keep it up, Red, and we're going to miss the opening altogether, because right now all I want to do is ravish you." He straightened his tie and sauntered toward her with his hands in his pockets, like some buff model straight off the runway.

His pseudo threat was pretty tempting, and pregnancy did have its perks as of late, but, in all seriousness, they did need to get over to the medical center soon. Today was her ribbon cutting. The Moira Garrity Family Wing was ready for its big debut. "Mmm," she hummed against his mouth, kissing him deeply. "Don't tempt me. Not today."

Maggie touched up her makeup while Finn called for a car, and then they were off to the heart of the city to finally see the completion of Maggie's dream come true. She'd invited young Emily to help with the cutting.

• • •

Maggie's speech was on fire. Finn admired the way she had with words. Her smile, her charisma—she lit up the room. The press surrounded her in the atrium of the hospital, their flashes bouncing off the walls with every shutter click. Emily stood beside her, up front and center—she'd been cancer free for almost a year and was the first person Maggie had thought of when it came time to schedule the grand opening. Finn had been happy to arrange the flights for her and her mother and pay for all expenses. The pure joy on Maggie's face was worth every penny, and when Emily and Maggie both held the giant scissors to ceremoniously cut the ribbon, his heart swelled with pride.

Maggie glanced over at him briefly and he smiled back. She'd done it. After answering a few questions, she made her way over to him, and he enveloped her in a hug. He inhaled her scent, the smell of the rooftop garden flowers lingering in her hair. "Congratulations," he whispered.

She looked up at him and smiled. "Thank you. For everything."

The side of his mouth twitched up into a half smile. "You ready to do this all over again next week in Maine?" He wrapped her in his arms, pulling her close.

She nodded. "Absolutely. And I can't wait to see my cat."

"I'm sure Tess is ready for you to see your cat. That thing hates her." Somehow, Maggie had talked his sister into cat-sitting whenever they were away. The thing loved Colin. Tess...not so much.

"Hate is such a strong word," she whispered, cringing.

He kissed her forehead. "We need to go pack for the flight. And don't forget about the surprise baby shower you don't know about, the one Nana and Tess have planned for Sunday." He'd let the surprise slip a few weeks ago on a lazy summer morning in bed, and Maggie hadn't let him live it down since. All jokes aside, he was looking forward to it. Everyone was coming over to the farm for a barbecue and baseball game in true Garrity tradition.

"Have you thought of any *real* names yet?" she asked.

"Hmm," he said, smiling. He laced his fingers in hers. "I was thinking... How do you feel about naming her Emily?"

Maggie rose up on her tippy-toes and planted a kiss on his lips. "I think it's perfect."

Acknowledgments

The Thank Yous...

There are so many people who made this book happen, who lifted me up and pushed me forward when I needed it. Anna, first and foremost, thank you for talking plot with me and always having the best ideas. To my editor, Robin, who has the patience of a saint—I couldn't have asked for a better first experience. You'll never know how grateful I am for your knowledge and quick replies to emails when I was freaking out over *all the things*. To my sister, Alexis, who listened to me ramble for hours about plot and character analysis during long drives and in school pickup lines and gave me childhood horror stories about us growing up on the ocean—*alone*—every summer... How did we survive? To my grandparents, who taught me how to love and laugh, and who raised me on lemonade, grilled cheese, and sunshine in my tiny coastal town in Maine. To Rockland and Rockport and the people within them who taught me how to fish, sail, and fully shell a lobstah—thank you for the kickass childhood. Not everyone is lucky enough to have the ocean for a backyard. I'm proud to call you home.

About the Author

Melissa spent her childhood exploring the coast of down east Maine without parental supervision and immersing herself in any book she could get her scrappy little hands on. Although she pursued a career in theater, the written word is her true calling. She leads a full life with her husband and six children traveling the country to wherever the Army sends them in her very large twelve-passenger van, in what she lovingly deems "organized chaos". She finds time to write in her "spare time", somewhere in between soccer practices and nap time. With coffee. Lots and lots of coffee. She loves creating unforgettable romance, and she enjoys writing and reading everything from sexy, sword-toting heroes to spit-out-your-coffee-funny romantic comedies... as long as she doesn't get the book wet. She leaves that up to the characters.

Find your Bliss with these great releases...

JUST ONE KISS
an Appletree Cove novel by Traci Hall

Free-spirited Grace Sheldon owes thirty thousand dollars on the house she's inherited. Her freelance photography definitely won't cover that. So, she opts for a temp job...at a dog training facility. Sawyer Rivera relishes his quiet life. Until his new office assistant, who knows more about chickens than the dogs he trains, comes crashing through his door. The woman is his complete opposite—and yet completely refreshing. Now Sawyer has one chance to try to change their fate before Grace's month of temp work is over.

THE KISS LIST
a Love List novel by Sonya Weiss

All Haley has ever wanted was her One True Love. Her parents knew they were soul mates at their first kiss, so surely Haley will, too, if she can just kiss each guy on her foolproof Kiss List. Enter Max: bane of Haley's existence but unfortunately, as a local, her way in with the guys. Max wants nothing to do with love or Haley, but the more time they spend together, the clearer it is that there's a paper-thin line between love and hate...

BETTING ON LOVE
a His Reason to Stay novel by Jennifer Hoopes

All Sam Ellis does is work. Concerned, his siblings bet he can't keep a girlfriend for thirty days. If he loses, he's out as CEO. No problem, he can fake a relationship. Whitney Carroll is back home in Gatlinburg, Tennessee after divorcing her low-down, cheating husband. Sam hires Whitney for a job and as his fake girlfriend. Their connection is undeniable but when disaster strikes, are they willing to trade their jobs for their hearts?